"Do you, Patrick, take Regina to be your wedded wife?"

Patrick let his mind wander as the judge droned on in a voice too loud for the stuffy little office in which the wedding was taking place. He didn't want to hear the ceremony anyway. If he didn't listen, taking the vow wouldn't be a lie.

He tried not to look next to him at Regina. Though he'd only known her forty-eight hours, she had a way of turning those large gray eyes on him and interrupting the impulses from his brain, of affecting his body's processes.

He'd come to Los Angeles to meet Wyatt Raleigh, single-minded in his purpose. He hadn't expected the solution to his financial problems to be a wife.

Patrick became suddenly aware that the room was silent and the judge was watching him expectantly. Beside him, Regina shifted again. He realized what they waited for.

He cleared his throat and said in a firm voice, "I do."

ABOUT THE AUTHOR

Muriel Jensen started writing in the sixth grade . . . and just never stopped. Marrying a journalist taught her the art of discipline and the playful art of arguing whether it's easier to get the "who, what, when, where and why" in the first paragraph or to take seventy thousand words in which to do it. Muriel Jensen lives in Astoria, Oregon, with her wonderful husband, two calico cats and a malamute named Deadline. She has three grown children.

Books by Muriel Jensen

HARLEQUIN AMERICAN ROMANCE

Don't miss any of our special offers. Write to us at the following address for information on our newest releases.

Harlequin Reader Service
P.O. Box 1397, Buffalo, NY 14240
Canadian address: P.O. Box 603,
Fort Erie, Ont. L2A 5X3

MURIEL JENSEN

MIDDLE OF THE RAINBOW

Harlequin Books

TORONTO • NEW YORK • LONDON
AMSTERDAM • PARIS • SYDNEY • HAMBURG
STOCKHOLM • ATHENS • TOKYO • MILAN
MADRID • WARSAW • BUDAPEST • AUCKLAND

Published November 1992

ISBN 0-373-16464-5

MIDDLE OF THE RAINBOW

Chapter One

"Do you, Patrick, take Regina to be your wedded wife? To have and to hold from this day forward, for better, for worse, for richer..."

Patrick let his mind wander as the judge droned on in a voice too loud for the stuffy little office in which the wedding was taking place. He didn't want to hear the ceremony, anyway. If he didn't listen, taking the vow wouldn't be a lie.

He tried not to look at Regina. Though he'd only known her forty-eight hours, she had a way of turning those large gray eyes on him and interrupting the impulses from his brain, of affecting his body's processes.

He felt her shoulder bump against his upper arm as she shifted her weight, heard the rustle of something silk under the soft blue dress she wore, filled his nostrils with her musk-and-magnolia scent with every breath he drew.

He'd come to Los Angeles to meet Wyatt Raleigh, single-minded in his purpose. He hadn't expected the solution to his financial problems to be a wife.

Patrick became suddenly aware that the room was silent and the judge was watching him expectantly. Beside him he felt Regina shift again. Behind him he heard the subtle cough of Paul Sinclair, his best man— the person who'd gotten him into this. He realized what they waited for.

"I do," he said firmly, clearly. He wasn't going to worry about it. She'd been as up-front as he had and they'd struck a deal.

Regina shifted again, this time losing her balance and falling hard against his arm. As the judge instinctively reached out for her, Patrick caught her hand and steadied her with an arm around her waist.

She glanced up at him with a wry little smile. "Sorry," she whispered, her eyes catching his for an instant before turning back to the judge.

"Do you, Regina, take Patrick for your wedded husband, to have and to hold from this day forward, for better..."

Get a grip! Gina warned herself. *You made a deal. So it all seemed less bizarre four days ago in your father's house than it does this morning in the judge's chambers. Remember that you'll get what you want, and that's what's important.*

As the judge's voice registered somewhere beyond her awareness, Gina tried to be comforted by that knowledge. But comfort had completely eluded her from the moment she'd read Patrick Gallagher's file.

She'd seen immediately that he was unlike anyone in her family or circle of friends. There was energy in the way he moved, excitement in his eyes.

He was perfect. But now as he stood beside her, tall, broad . . . and proprietary, she wondered if she'd gotten in over her head.

PATRICK COULD FEEL her losing her nerve. The hand he held was shaking. He firmed his grip, wanting to get through this before she changed her mind.

The outrageousness of the deal they'd struck had hit him that morning when he'd been shaving, but he had too much to lose . . . and a roll of the dice was worth the gamble.

IT HAD ALL BEGUN as a request for a loan from a financier with a reputation for bold investment. Of course, approaching Wyatt Raleigh had been Sin's idea. Patrick could only blame himself for forgetting that anything involving his buddy, Paul Sinclair, deserved careful consideration. But he hadn't had time.

He'd driven from Candle Bay, Oregon, to Sin's place in Malibu. He'd have preferred to fly, but driving his long-bed truck would allow him to pick up the double oak doors for the hotel's main entrance from a Southern Oregon craftsman.

"Why don't you just let *me* lend you the money?" Sin had asked as they'd had drinks on a redwood deck overlooking the ocean while a colorful sunset bloomed out of it.

They'd had that argument three days earlier on the phone. "I told you. If I lose everything, I don't want it to be your money."

"It wouldn't matter."

"It would to me."

Sin glanced away from the horizon. "It's only money, Pat," he said with a grin.

Patrick laughed. "Spoken like a man with an endless supply. Thanks, but I'll take my chances with Wyatt Raleigh. He knows I'm coming?"

Sin nodded. "I confirmed this morning."

The following afternoon, Sin's classic Pininfarina had wound its way into a hilly, wooded area that had surprised Patrick with its rustic remoteness. Sin had dropped him off in front of a modern, multilevel house fitted on a slope like an angular bird. "Be back for you in a couple of hours," he'd said. "Good luck."

A small brunette in an apron answered the door. She studied Patrick, an eyebrow raised in question.

"I'm Patrick Gallagher," he said. "I have an appointment with Mr. Raleigh."

She gave him a slow, once-over glance, then opened the door wide and stepped aside. Another time, he might have returned the glance, but now he had other things on his mind. He followed her up a blue-carpeted, oak-banistered staircase to a hallway lined with Ron Jensen seascapes. She rapped twice on a door at the end of the hall, pushed it open, smiled at him and turned back the way they'd come.

A tall, slender man in tennis whites came across the paneled study, hand extended. He was fit, with thinning gray hair and wire-rimmed glasses. He moved like Sin did, Patrick noted, with a grace that spoke of breeding.

"Mr. Raleigh," Patrick said. "I'm Patrick Gallagher."

"Welcome to Los Angeles," Raleigh said, leading Patrick to a chair that faced his desk. "Can I get you a drink?"

"A gin and tonic, please."

Raleigh went to a small bar across the study and was back in a moment carrying two frosty glasses with twists of lime.

"Sinclair tells me this has something to do with a hotel that's been in your family for some time. Please. Sit down."

"The Candle Bay Inn," Patrick replied, easing into the soft cordovan leather. "Near the mouth of the Columbia. My great-grandfather built it at the turn of the century."

Raleigh took his chair behind the desk and nodded with interest. "Queen Anne architecture. Eighty rooms. You're talking about adding charter boats, tours of historic Astoria and a new chef."

Good. He was dealing with a man who did his research. "If you know all that," Patrick said, "you must also know that I'm taking over for my grandfather, who just passed away. Because the bank doesn't know me..."

Raleigh nodded again. "Because you've spent the last ten years in the military. You've been a civilian only six months. Go on."

Patrick calmly continued. "Because the bank doesn't know me, they're calling in the loan my grandfather took out to remodel and expand. The job's only half-done. Without remodeling, we can no longer provide the comfort people look for in a hotel, and without expanding we won't be able to compete with the bigger houses in Seaside or on the Washington peninsula."

"You've talked to the bank?" Raleigh asked. "You've explained to them you grew up in the business?" He smiled slowly. "Explained that if you can take care of a company of young marines, you can do anything in this world you set your mind to?"

Patrick grinned. "Did your stint in the corps?"

"In the Navy, actually, but we had the standard marine contingent aboard ship. They were fearless on duty and reckless on leave. Tough bunch to command."

Patrick nodded. "The bank wants to see my experience on a profit-and-loss statement." He shrugged. "I can't give them that. I hoped you'd be more openminded."

"I might be. Tell me your plans."

For an hour Patrick explained what he wanted to do with the Candle Bay Inn. The bed-and-breakfast certainly fulfilled a need, but many people wanted more than the usual room, shared bath, and croissants and coffee that the standard B&B provided.

"The Candle Bay Inn doesn't provide day care for guests' children yet, but that's something I'm working on," Patrick said, downing the last of his drink. "But I know I can fill every other need if I can finish the remodeling and the addition. Right now I've got a crew of carpenters standing around, eating up money. If I let them go until the money problem's ironed out, they'll go to work for somebody else. It's already late April. I'll lose the season."

Raleigh nodded thoughtfully as he refilled Patrick's empty glass. "I might be able to help you," he said.

Patrick drew the first even breath he'd taken since Sin had dropped him off.

"After looking into your background," Raleigh said, freshening his own drink, then walking back to his chair, "I thought you seemed like a good bet." He moved his glass in a circular, stirring motion and smiled. "That's all a loan is, you know—a sort of bet on an individual. I never lend on the basis of a company's figures, but on the track record of the man guiding it. Now that I've met you, I'm convinced you'll give it everything you have."

He took a long drink, put his glass down on a notepad on his desk, then leaned back in his chair and laced his fingers over his stomach. He met Patrick's eyes. "But we both know that however good you are, lending you the amount of money you've asked for is still a risk.''

Patrick nodded. "Yes, it is."

There was a long pause. Patrick waited. Then Raleigh said suddenly, "I'm willing to take it. But there is a condition."

Patrick's mind ran through the conditions a man of Raleigh's reputation might attach to a business deal. He couldn't think of one he wouldn't be willing to meet.

"Name it," he said.

Raleigh picked up his drink, took another swallow, then put it down again. "I'd like you to take my daughter back to Oregon with you—as your wife."

For a moment Patrick could only wonder if he'd heard correctly. When Raleigh nodded in silent reply to his unspoken question, Patrick felt as though he were holding a grenade in one hand and its pin in the other; he had to think fast or he was going to get his head blown off.

"Why?" he asked. Not a brilliant tactic, but bound to produce important answers and buy him time.

Raleigh smiled again. "Not prone to panic. I like that. Because she's been in one scrape after the other ever since she graduated from college."

"Scrape?"

"Oh, nothing serious until this last thing with Yale Gardner. But she likes her friends a little wild. She's often in the tabloid headlines. Dancing in the fountain at the music center, being the cause of a brawl at some yuppy watering hole, picketing city hall because they were bullied into taking down an art show that contained nudes.''

That all sounded pretty tame to Patrick. ''Who's Yale Gardner?''

Raleigh sighed with paternal frustration. ''Two years ago she insisted on opening a design firm with a friend of hers from art school. I tried to warn her, but she wouldn't listen. Sank every penny into it.'' He raised both hands in a philosophical gesture. ''Lost it all a month ago when her partner—'' he emphasized the word scornfully ''—stole jewels, antiques and artwork from their clients, raided their savings account and took off for parts unknown. She had to liquidate to try to make restitution to her clients. Now she doesn't have a dime until she comes into her inheritance from her grandmother when she turns twenty-six next March.''

Patrick couldn't help the instinctive glance at his opulent surroundings. ''You couldn't help her?''

Raleigh shook his head adamantly. ''I told her, when she insisted on ignoring my warnings, that I wasn't going to bail her out when she got into trouble again. A parent has to stand firm.''

''But you can't blame her for her partner's—''

''I can blame her for trusting every freeloader who comes along,'' Raleigh interrupted. ''I can blame her for refusing to listen to sound advice. What I *am* going to do for her is take an old-world father approach and find a husband for her.''

"Mr. Raleigh," Patrick said calmly, "I'm up to my neck in problems and debt. I—"

"I can solve the debt problems," Raleigh interrupted.

Patrick could almost see a wheelbarrow filled with cash rolling away from him. "You can't bargain marriage with money," he said, although considering the desperation with which he wanted to save the Candle Bay Inn, he wasn't absolutely sure of that. "At least . . . you shouldn't."

"Oh, I'm not," Raleigh assured him with an innocent smile. "I've been looking for the right man everywhere. You're the only one with all the qualifications."

"And those are?"

"Toughness, tenacity, ingenuity, honesty."

Patrick shook his head and grinned at the impressive list of attributes. "Mr. Raleigh, you may know my background, but you don't know me. I—"

"The corps had a pretty detailed psychological profile on you. I hate to contradict you, but I think I do know you."

Patrick unbuttoned his jacket and leaned back in his chair. He had a feeling the rest of this interview was going to require some quick moves on his part.

"Regina's mother died when she was a baby," Raleigh explained with sudden sobriety. "I was very busy and didn't make enough time for my daughter or her brothers. The boys eventually came to work for me, but Gina's a right-brained kind of person—all feeling and artistic emotion. Bad qualities in an investor.''

Patrick nodded.

''The minute she came into her trust at twenty-one she left the house. She supported every underdog that happened by. Then she took up with all her strange friends and went into business with Gardner. I watched all the money I worked so hard to give her go down the drain.''

Raleigh's voice had risen, and Patrick could see that the notorious Regina had almost managed to crease her father's calm. Then he drew a breath and straightened in his chair.

''I'm within a week of launching my campaign for Congress, and I won't get very far with her making the headlines twice a week.''

So, that was it. Patrick was desperate for Raleigh's money, but not hard-up enough to coerce a young woman into marriage to further her father's political career.

He stood and carried his glass to the bar. Then he turned and faced Raleigh across the desk. ''Thank you for your time and your interest, but I'm having enough trouble serving my own ambitions. I can't serve yours, too. I'll see myself out.''

''You misunderstand me, Gallagher,'' Raleigh said. ''Regina is not unwilling.''

That stopped Patrick halfway to the door. He couldn't help a surprised ''She isn't?''

"No," Raleigh replied, picking up a Mont Blanc pen and turning it thoughtfully in his fingers. "And that should give us both pause. But, for reasons of her own, Regina is perfectly willing to consider you as a husband."

Patrick absorbed that information and continued to the door. He stopped and turned with his hand on the ornate brass pull. "Thank you again, but if she's comparison shopping, I'm sure I'm not her man. Or yours."

"Wouldn't you like to meet her first?"

"No, thank you." Patrick opened the door and found the little brunette maid on the other side, her hand raised and prepared to knock.

Large gray eyes pinned him in place.

She no longer wore the apron but black leggings and a long yellow sweater. She looked into his eyes, apparently trying to read his expression.

"Hi," she said tentatively. He began to entertain a nagging suspicion.

"Regina," he guessed.

"Yes, Patrick." She folded her arms and asked anxiously, "You're not leaving?"

Raleigh was on his feet behind the desk. "You two have met?"

Patrick shook his head, casting her a scolding glance. "Not precisely. She let me in, pretending to be the maid."

"I let you in wearing an apron," she corrected with a smile. "You *assumed* I was the maid."

They stared at each other. Patrick liked to pride himself on the ability to read people and situations and find the most expedient way to deal with both.

She had thick, dark hair that reached her shoulders, and bangs that were swept to the side in a fanlike swoosh. She was average in height, small but roundly built, with a challenging angle in her shoulders and chin.

Something in him responded. "I was leaving," he heard himself say. He'd have sworn *I am leaving* was the impulse his brain had sent to his tongue. He fought to regain ground. "I understand you're considering marriage to me, but so far your father's explained that you're troublesome, quarrelsome and an exhibitionist. Is there something you'd like to add to that to make the notion more appealing to me?"

"MISS RALEIGH!" The judge's urgent whisper made Gina look up at Patrick. Now he was waiting for *her* answer and she wasn't sure she knew what to say. Could this possibly work? Granted, it had to work for less than a year, but that could seem like an eternity.

She was aware of the pulsing silence in the room. She was also conscious of the strong arm around her waist still lending support. She drew a deep breath and said strongly, "I do."

IN HER FATHER'S STUDY Regina considered Patrick Gallagher. So his polished civility was just a veneer.

Considering her situation, that could be a good thing. "Would you like to talk in the garden?" she asked.

"Come on, Gallagher," her father prodded Patrick hopefully. "Can't hurt."

Patrick glanced doubtfully at him then back at her. He finally swept a hand toward the door, indicating that she should lead the way.

He kept abreast of her down the stairs and through the French doors in the kitchen to the velvet stretch of lawn behind the house. A colorful border of flowers, birds of paradise pointing their orange heads inward, surrounded it. She drew in a sweet breath and felt herself relax a little.

She led him to a canopied redwood picnic table. She slid into one side and he straddled the other. She looked up at him, prepared to make a laughing remark about the unusual circumstances, and found his dark gaze measuring and faintly disapproving.

"All right, so I'm not a bargain," she said candidly. "I'm rich and spoiled and like things my own way. I'm not much good in the out-of-doors with Mother Nature. But I could adjust."

He appeared unmoved by her candor. "Why are you doing this?" he asked without preamble. "Why would a pretty, intelligent woman let her father manipulate her this way? You don't want to go to work, is that it? You can't make an honest buck?"

She couldn't blame him for assuming that. "Not at the moment," she answered quietly. "At least, not in what I'm trained to do. My reputation in business has been destroyed.''

''So you'd rather marry a stranger?''

She suddenly found it difficult to meet his eyes. She looked up at the underside of the yellow-and-white striped canopy. ''Actually,'' she said, ''I agreed to my father's suggestion because I have my own agenda ... and my own thoughts on how a marriage between us could be conducted.''

When he said nothing, she lowered her eyes to his. He was removing his jacket. ''Please,'' he said with a dry, sideways glance at her. ''Elaborate. I can hardly wait.''

She watched big shoulders ripple under his white shirt as he yanked the tie off and tossed it onto the jacket on the bench. Then he leaned on an elbow and gave her his attention.

She felt her mouth go dry. She decided to tell him the easy part first. ''In eleven months,'' she said, folding her arms on the table, ''I'll be twenty-six and come into the money my grandmother left me. It'll be more than enough to pay back the rest of what I owe my clients and start over again.''

He frowned. ''Then why not just wait for your inheritance?''

She made a point of keeping her eyes down, her voice casual. ''Because I don't have a dime until then. You'd only have to put up with me for eleven months, then I'd walk out of your life forever.'' She grinned at him, but his expression didn't change. "I have another reason," she added seriously.

He was quiet for a long moment. "What?" he asked.

She'd had every intention of telling him the truth, but she knew what he would say: call the police; hire a private investigator. He was studying her across the table with a look of moral superiority—as though he was a man of purpose and direction forced to waste time with a silly young woman.

She quickly changed tack and decided to tell him another truth that would shock him.

"I want a baby," she said calmly.

For a long moment he stared at her. A breeze rippled through the fan palm at the other end of the lawn, insects hummed, and somewhere in the distance birds chattered. Then Patrick gathered up his coat and tie and started back toward the house. She caught him in the middle of the deep expanse of lawn.

"Hear me out," she pleaded, looping her arm in his so that he was forced to stop or drag her.

He came to a halt impatiently, looking down at her with an expression that brought color to her cheeks. This was not the reaction she'd expected, but she doubted he would believe the truth. And wanting a baby wasn't a lie. The perfect father had just never presented himself before.

"Where I come from," he said firmly, "we still cherish the traditional values. Babies are born out of love, not as a condition of a loan."

"I just thought," she said, trying not to sound desperate, "that I could help you and you could help me."

"I don't need a spoiled, selfish wife. I already have enough problems. I came to your father hoping to relieve some of them, not acquire new ones."

"Did I mention," she went on intrepidly, "that I'm a pretty good cook, I give a great back rub, and I'm good at staying out of the way?"

"Why," he demanded, annoyed by the fact that there was something touching about her persistence, "would you want a baby when you just suggested we go our separate ways in eleven months?"

"Because I've lived my whole life," she replied without hesitation, "alone and lonely. My father was always busy. My brothers are just like him. I love them but I want someone who is mine."

"People," he said in a gently admonishing tone, "don't belong to other people."

She nodded and sighed. "Apparently. Even those who brought you into their world."

Patrick ran a hand down his face. "I'm sorry," he said. "I've talked to your father and I think I understand what you're saying. But I've lived hard all over the world, and I've maintained a certain ... standard for my own behavior, which includes not impregnating women with whom I do not plan to spend the rest of my life.''

She put a hand on his arm and saw something in his eyes react. ''Patrick...'' she began.

He grasped her wrist in his free hand and removed it. ''There have to be a dozen blue bloods around here who would be happy to oblige you.''

She stood still in his grasp and met his eyes. ''I have a standard of my own, and that is not to make a baby with a jerk. I've read your file, too. I know what you're made of.''

He dropped his jacket on the ground and pushed her down beside it, sitting knee to knee with her, his grip still firm. ''You have no idea what I'm made of. I work long hours and I have a short temper. Married to me, you'd find yourself alone sixteen hours of the day unless you can wield a hammer, run a front desk or create a day-care facility that...''

He stopped midsentence as her whole countenance brightened. ''A day-care facility? At your hotel? I could do that! Patrick, I could do that. I took classes in early-childhood education. I know all about...''

He released her and got to his feet. She sprang up beside him. They looked into each other's eyes, he undecided, she hopeful.

Then he reached under her hair to shape her head in his hand. His dark eyes warned her he was up to something. She felt her breath stop as he lowered his head.

"Don't you even want to know if you'll like it with me first?" he asked softly. He opened his mouth over hers and gave her a kiss that wasn't hesitant or exploratory or polite. It was a kiss intended to frighten her off.

He held her immobile, his tongue probed deeply, and his free hand ran down her back, over her hip, then up again.

Everything in her responded and quickened: heartbeat, bloodstream, nervous system. She felt strength in him and the suggestion of a powerful passion.

When he tugged her head back to look into her eyes, his were dark with surprise.

She dragged in a gulp of air and smiled up at him. "Yes," she said, her voice breathless. "I think I will."

He stared at her for one interminable moment, and she braced herself for his refusal. Then he leaned over her, still gripping her hair, until they were nose to nose.

"The first time you whine about the bad weather," he warned, "my long hours, the disrepair of the house or the lack of entertainment, I'm sending you back to your father fourth-class mail. Is that clear?"

Elation filled her, but she had the sense to look meek. "Yes," she replied.

"And the baby issue is not resolved."

"I want—" she began huffily.

He cut her off with a quiet but final "No. I'll marry you to keep you out of trouble until you come into your inheritance. In exchange, you will set up child care at the inn. That's the deal."

Gina was tempted to argue. But she'd felt that flare of passion. Maybe she didn't have to.

"Fine," she submitted.

"Good," he said, releasing her as he straightened. Then he closed his eyes and shook his head, and added, "I hope."

Chapter Two

"By the power invested in me by the State of California, I now pronounce you man and wife."

Gina drew a breath and turned to Patrick as the judge smiled. *Past the point of no return,* she thought. *I can do this.*

Patrick leaned down to give her a chaste kiss. *You've done it, Gallagher,* he congratulated himself. *You have the money. 'Course, you also have a wife.*

As she kissed him back, sweetly but with that suggestion of need he'd felt in her four days ago on her lawn, he was a little confused to find himself more fascinated with her than with the check in his pocket.

"YOU ARE CERTIFIABLE!" Bobbi Perducci, Gina's maid-of-honor, said as they stood in front of a bank of makeup mirrors in the ladies' room of the Woodland Restaurant. "You should have a box at the funny farm, life membership in the bin! You—"

"I get the message, Bobbi," Gina said, smoothing the hem of a pink sweater over matching tights. The wedding party had changed clothes, packed Patrick's canopied blue-and-silver Chevy truck, then found a quiet place for lunch before going their separate ways—Patrick and Gina north to Oregon, Sin back to his law practice and Bobbi back to her small furniture-restoration shop.

Gina kneaded the area behind her ears, hoping to relieve the tension there.

Bobbi stopped her diatribe to ask solicitously, "You want an aspirin?"

"Oh, please."

Bobbi delved into a small leather bag and produced a piece of round, red plastic that telescoped into a cup with aspirin secured in its lid. Gina shook her head over her friend's preparedness.

"I don't know what I'd do without you, Bobbi," Gina said as she palmed two aspirin and held the cup under running water.

"I don't know what I'd do without you, either," Bobbi said, watching frowningly in the mirror while Gina tossed the aspirin into her mouth and swallowed. "So please be careful. What did Patrick say when you told him about the . . . ?"

"Nothing." Gina tore a hand towel from the dispenser and avoided the mirror as she wiped the cup. "I haven't told him."

"You haven't—" Bobbi gasped. "Regina Jane, what is *wrong* with you?"

Gina handed the cup back and smiled. "Well, Barbara Elizabeth, I'll tell you. The gentleman doesn't like to be used, and he was feeling pretty put-upon already."

Bobbi rolled her eyes. "Well, big surprise. Didn't I tell you this was crazy? What man would dare take on a wife just to get a loan?"

Gina brushed her hair, feeling the tension begin to loosen. It *was* crazy, but she'd done it. That was all that counted. "A man from Oregon, apparently. He put up a little resistance, laid down a few rules, then agreed."

"Because you didn't tell him the truth."

"I did. Just not all of it. But I will."

"You'd better make it fast. I'm sure it's Yale Gardner, or something to do with him. He probably wants to frighten you into keeping quiet about what he's stolen from you."

"Well, he's too late," Gina said. "I've already told the police everything I know."

"Maybe he wants retribution."

A little frisson of fear tried to shake Gina's new calm, but she refused to let it. "I'll be somewhere on Highway 101 with a two-hundred-pound ex-marine who has a vested interest in my personal safety."

Bobbi shook her head helplessly. "Gina, it won't be that simple. You should—"

"Bobbi," Gina said firmly, dropping her brush into her purse and turning her friend toward the rest-room door. "This is my wedding day. Though it came about in an unorthodox way, I'd like to enjoy it. Don't spoil it for me, okay?"

Bobbi turned at the door with a dreamy sigh. "He does have wonderful shoulders. Maybe something will come..."

Gina reached around her to pull open the door and push her gently through. "Snagging him was miracle enough. Thinking he might want to keep me when this is over is too much to hope for."

Besides, she thought as she followed Bobbi back toward their table, she was already beginning to wonder who'd snagged whom.

IN A CHINTZ-COVERED booth in a dining room decorated like a French country house, Sin looked at Patrick over his menu. "Can I have a drink?" he asked. "Or do I have to be on my best behavior?"

Patrick folded his menu and put it down. "Your best behavior is acceptable only around campfires on the John Day River, or possibly in the Sing Sing cafeteria."

Sin slapped his menu on top of Patrick's. "That's the thanks I get for coming through for you. Do you have another friend who could find you half a million dollars and a beautiful woman on a few days' notice?"

"I appreciate your putting the loan together," Patrick said, signaling the waitress. "I don't recall asking for a wife. You can have one drink. You have to drive Bobbi home when we leave."

Sin ordered a bottle of champagne, then leaned back in the booth and studied his friend with a thoughtful expression. "I didn't know Raleigh was going to make his daughter a condition of the loan. I guess I did too good a job selling you to him. My mistake. Actually, I think this'll be good for you."

Patrick raised an inquiring eyebrow. "How so?"

"Because you're so...military." Sin laughed lightly and shook his head. "Of course, if it hadn't been for your early-rising, schedule-keeping, everything-planned-in-detail approach to things, I'd never have graduated. But it was hell being your roommate. Go easy on Gina, okay? I like her."

Patrick sent a dark glance in the direction in which the girls had disappeared. He could still smell magnolias beside him. "She agreed to marry a man she doesn't know, to serve her own purposes."

Sin nodded and studied him levelly. "Isn't that what you're doing?"

"I'm trying to save a beautiful old inn that four generations of my family have loved and dedicated their lives to."

"Why's she doing it?"

Patrick hesitated. He'd trust Paul Sinclair with everything he had including his life, but he divulged only half Gina's reason. He wasn't sure if he did it out of deference to her privacy or his unwillingness to be part of her baby plan.

"I told you about the thing with her business partner." Sin nodded. "Well, she's flat broke, and her father refuses to help. He pawned her off on me until an inheritance from her grandmother becomes hers on her twenty-sixth birthday.''

''When is that?''

''Next March. Her plan is that we...help each other out for eleven months. Then both of us will have what we want.''

''You haven't made any dumb marriage-of-convenience agreements, like separate beds or anything like that?''

''No.'' Patrick reached for his water glass and studied it earnestly. ''Quite the opposite, in fact.''

Sin leaned forward in grinning interest. ''Really? Want to elaborate?''

Patrick gave him a studied look and shook his head. ''No. It's all very complex, but it's less than a year. I can handle it.''

''Just another skirmish,'' Sin said knowingly. ''You think this is going to be like any other battle where all you have to do is go in armed and ready and determined to be tougher than the enemy.''

''Don't knock it,'' Patrick said. ''It works.''

Sin leaned toward him earnestly. ''It works on other men. It does not work on women. Dealing with a woman that way would be like...like sending a military band to deal with guerrillas. She'll clean your clock.'' He straightened and grinned. ''Then again, I think that could be a good thing. You need loosening up.''

"So I can be like you?" Patrick challenged. "Going from woman to woman, looking for what you can't find because your life-style is *too* loose?"

Something altered subtly in Sin's eyes, and Patrick immediately regretted the gibe. He knew better than anyone why Sin was the way he was.

"Look, I—" he began.

"What I meant was," Sin interrupted him, dismissing any suggestion of hurt feelings with a swipe of his hand, "you might get something out of this. Relax and let yourself feel something." He paused and added quietly, seriously, "She has feelings for you."

"You're crazy."

"I can see it in her eyes."

"If that were true, it would only be because I can give her what she wants for a year."

"Because she needs something you have," Sin corrected with uncharacteristic gravity. "I recognize the look. I'll wager she was raised just like I was—alone. She needs a friend—just like I did."

The subject was dropped as the waiter arrived with a champagne bucket. The women returned to the table as the waiter popped the cork.

Patrick watched Gina laughing with Bobbi and felt that strange disruption she consistently caused in him. For a man whose entire adult life had required a brain and a body that functioned sharply and in harmony, the reaction was upsetting.

Then she turned to him, still laughing as Sin leaned across Bobbi and said something that made even the waiter laugh. She raised her glass, her expression sobering as her eyes met his.

He saw the look Sin had talked about—had seen it four days ago when they'd met. He didn't understand it, wasn't even sure he wanted to be needed in the way the look suggested, but he'd promised, and he took his responsibilities seriously.

He raised his glass in response, smiling. Her eyes brightened. Four glasses clinked together over the middle of the table. "To Gina and Patrick," Sin said, "and much happiness."

"To the middle of the rainbow," Bobbi said.

Sin lowered his glass and frowned at her. "The middle? Isn't the traditional wish for what lies in the pot of gold at the *end* of the rainbow?"

"Gina doesn't think so," Bobbi explained. "Her family has the pot of gold, and it's not what it's…cracked up to…be." She faltered as Gina caught her eye with a faintly embarrassed glance. "Well, there's nothing wrong with that," Bobbi said defensively. "I think you've got the right idea." She looked from Sin to Patrick. "She always says that getting what you want is like sitting on top, right in the middle of the bow."

Sin smiled at Gina and raised his glass again. "As another resident of the 'pot,' I concur. To the middle of the rainbow."

Glasses clinked again and everyone drank a toast.

"Are you going to take time and honeymoon along the way?" Sin asked.

"No time," Patrick said, giving him a dirty look. "All my crews are back to work. I should be there to supervise."

"So you're driving up the middle? Interstate 5?"

Patrick shook his head. "No, 101. I have to pick up new oak doors for the main building."

Sin closed his eyes and shook his head. "You're going to travel the California and Oregon coasts, a thousand miles of the most beautiful scenery God ever made, and I'll bet you'll still keep to a schedule."

"We're both anxious to get to Candle Bay," Gina said quietly.

Patrick saw the quick glance Bobbi sent Gina that Gina returned with the bland arch of an eyebrow. When she glanced his way and found him watching her, something disturbed the careful neutrality in her eyes and he saw something secretive there. Then she smiled at him and turned her attention to the menu.

THE GIRLS HUGGED goodbye while Sin and Patrick leaned patiently on the truck's front fender.

"God, I hope they don't start crying," Sin said. "I don't know how to handle it when they cry. And I have to take Bobbi home."

"Well, here's your opportunity to offer sympathy and comfort and turn her mood into one you know you can deal with."

Sin gave him a wry glance. "Don't get condescending with me because you're taking a wife home and not a stranger."

Patrick elbowed him and grinned. "Come on, you've never met a stranger. I think she likes you already."

Sin turned to study Bobbi with a narrowed glance as she and Gina walked arm in arm toward the truck. "Interesting woman," he said thoughtfully.

Patrick thought he could agree, though Sin found all women interesting. He straightened away from the fender as the girls joined them. They both looked a little grim, he thought. He'd observed how close they were that morning and how much they meant to each other.

Instinctively he put an arm around Gina as she came to stand beside him.

"Sin's coming to visit for the inn's yearly Memorial Day Weekend celebration," he said, surprised by the need to make her smile. "He could bring Bobbi with him if she can take the time."

He was rewarded when the girls exchanged hopeful smiles, and Gina looked up at him with gratitude. "I'd love that," she said.

He opened the passenger-side door and put her into the truck. Then he turned to give Bobbi a quick hug.

"You take good care of Gina," she said gravely, sounding a little, he thought, as though he were taking her off to war.

"I will," he promised. "And in exchange, I want you to keep an eye on Sin for me. He tends to get into trouble."

Bobbi looked from one man to the other. "What kind of trouble?"

Sin unashamedly wrapped his arms around Patrick. "You should talk," he said under his breath. "Which one of us ended up married?" Then he stepped back and clapped Patrick on the shoulder. "Take care. Call if you need legal advice."

"Right." Patrick climbed into the cab of the truck, backed out of the parking lot, then waved with Gina as he moved slowly toward the street. A final glimpse into the rearview mirror as he pulled out into the traffic showed Bobbi turning tearfully into Sin's shoulder and his arms closing around her. He guessed that in a matter of minutes Sin would have Gina's friend smiling once again.

PATRICK CONCENTRATED on the traffic as he turned onto the freeway. He waited until he'd slipped into the stream of cars moving sixty-five miles an hour before he glanced at Gina. She was staring moodily out the side window.

"Regrets?" he asked.

She turned to him, an eyebrow raised. "No. You?"

He shook his head. "I'm the one with a check in my pocket."

"And a wife."

"I'm assuming there'll be advantages to that as well as responsibilities."

She shifted, turning to face him. He heard the smile in her voice as he concentrated on the traffic.

"I told you that I'm a good cook, but don't count on breakfast because I'm a sack rat. Nothing happens that I care about before 8:00 a.m."

He checked the mirror to pass a pickup losing a top layer of trash and slid her a grin as he maneuvered. "Breakfast is my favorite meal. Do we need a counselor already?"

"Of course not," she said amiably. "You can fix it for me, and I'll prepare the other two meals. What time are you up?"

"Five-thirty," he replied, relaxing as the traffic moved comfortably.

She made a little sound of distress and teased, "You can just leave me something I can microwave." She added as an afterthought, "Do we have a microwave?"

"We do. The house is equipped with all the conveniences, it's just that the structure itself was built in 1887 and needs a lot of work. The plumbing and wiring are in desperate need of updating, too. On a scale of one to ten, if your father's place is a ten, mine's about a two."

"I make a point of ignoring scales of all kinds," she said, then she daintily covered her mouth and gave a great yawn.

He glanced away from the road to let his eyes run the length of her trim body in amazement. "No wonder. That was quite a lunch you packed away. You didn't tell me you have an appetite like a longshoreman."

"There's a lot I haven't told you," she said, finding a weird kind of relief in the veiled honesty. She batted her eyelashes at him. "A woman has to maintain an air of mystery, you know. Otherwise, what's to keep you interested? Although I don't suppose a marine wants that kind of a woman, does he? I mean, as a former officer in the corps, you would probably look for a woman who can take orders and hop to."

He considered that a moment, then inclined his head in a casual gesture. "As a former officer in the corps," he replied, "I know how to make anyone, woman or marine, do what I want whether they're willing to or not. In fact, the challenge of going head to head—" there was a brief, suggestive pause "—or whatever is at issue . . . is more satisfying than an easy victory."

Something inside her was warned and excited at the same time. "Have you ever had a serious relationship?"

"No," he replied. "No time. Six months here, a year there. It doesn't make for lasting liaisons."

She yawned again.

"Why don't you doze for a couple of hours," he suggested. "We'll stop for the night near San Luis Obispo."

"You can go farther if you want to." She tried to sound casual, without motive. "I know you're in a hurry to get there."

"Another few hours won't make much difference."

"You need help navigating or anything?"

"No. We'll stay on 101 all the way."

"If you're sure." She leaned down in her seat, then turned to grin at him. "You promise to wake me when you stop for dinner?"

He had to grin back. "You're not thinking about dinner already?"

She tucked her feet up on the seat and took the jacket he'd discarded between them and put it over her. "I'm always wondering about my next meal. Must be some primal thing that harkens back to my great-great-grandfather Raleigh who lost everything in a drought. He and his family ate nothing but potatoes and root vegetables one whole winter." She shuddered dramatically, then yawned again. "I can tolerate anything as long as I have a bag of potato chips and shortbread cookies."

"Between meals."

"Right." She sounded as though she was already drifting.

He glanced her way. A wave of dark hair fell over her cheek; her eyelashes lay against its pallor, impossibly dark and long; and her lips, pink and full, pursed together as though some troublesome dream had already claimed her.

He reached out to draw the jacket up when it slipped off the slope of her shoulder. She snuggled into it, and her frown turned to a smile. Unable to stop himself, he rubbed a knuckle along her satin cheek. He was suddenly consumed with wondering if her skin would feel like that everywhere.

He had to drag his mind back to the traffic to avoid driving up the back of the trash-laden pickup that had somehow gotten ahead of him again. Regina Raleigh, he thought, then corrected himself—Regina Gallagher—could be dangerous to his health.

He had no idea how prophetic the thought was.

Chapter Three

It was twilight. San Luis Obispo stretched out along the purple hills, strung with neon signs and street- and traffic lights. The night was balmy, the air perfumed with orange blossoms from an orchard that dotted one of the hills in a perfectly symmetrical pattern. Gina, who had just awakened, smiled at the fragrance. Orange blossoms, the classic wedding flower. Nature was teasing her.

Gina looked at the man beside her. In a navy blue cotton sweater and jeans, his dark hair rakishly disturbed by his open window, he looked like an ad for every woman's preconceived notion of the Northwest man. Sometime while she'd been asleep, he'd rolled up the sleeves of the sweater, revealing sturdy forearms that reacted as he controlled the wheel.

She could envision those biceps under a plaid shirt, chopping wood or reeling in a net gorged with fish. A plain gold band on his left hand matched the wider band on hers. Married, she thought in renewed wonder. She was married to him.

On the heels of that realization, she suddenly thought of lying in arms that had never held her, under hands that had never touched her. She was simultaneously eager to know what it would be like to make love with Patrick Gallagher and appalled that she'd used such means to get what she needed.

"You *are* a sack rat," Patrick observed as he turned the car into the driveway of a large motel whose marquee boasted a maximum of comfort and a minimum of noise.

Unsettled by her thoughts, Gina looked at him blankly for a moment.

He pulled up in front of the office and turned off the motor, frowning at her vaguely alarmed expression.

"You all right?" he asked.

She nodded quickly. "Just disoriented. What time is it?"

"Ten of seven. You slept quite a while. This doesn't mean you'll be watching midnight movies and racking up cable charges on the hotel television, does it?"

He was testing the waters. She looked nervous suddenly, and he was surprised. She'd been so matter-of-fact about the baby thing, so unconcerned that lovemaking would be a part of their relationship.

She smiled, but even on such short acquaintance, he knew it wasn't genuine. "No," she answered. "I spent most of last night packing and taking care of last-minute business. That was catch-up sleep."

The lady was frightened, he decided. That didn't upset him. It almost made her seem more normal.

"Want to come inside with me?" he asked. "Or wait in the car?"

"I'll wait," she said.

As he disappeared inside the office, she leaned back in her seat with a ragged sigh. God. She should have stayed awake. She should have been watching. She looked around at the cars already parked for the night in the huge lot around which the motel was built. No black Mercedes. She twisted in her seat to look over her shoulder.

Traffic sped past on the town's main thoroughfare. Nothing seemed out of the ordinary.

Patrick slipped into the truck and she started guiltily, as though her thoughts were written on her forehead.

"Relax," he said with a grin, dropping their room key into her lap. "I promise to beat you only with a little stick."

She returned his grin, hoping he'd hold to that promise when and if he ever found out why she'd really married him.

The room was spacious and immaculate. Gina's discomfort swelled. Patrick had placed their bags on the foot of the king-size bed and was reading a visitor's guide on the counter beside the television. *I should tell him,* she thought. *It would be so easy to just say it now.*

"We have Mexican food, Chinese food, French cuisine, seafood, barbecue and any number of fast-food restaurants." He turned to her before she could speak. "What sounds good?"

He was very large she realized, studying him in the concentration of light from a wall lamp near his head, very thick in the shoulders, very lean in the hips. From the lamp his dark hair picked up bourbon-colored highlights. His cheekbones and jaw were sharply defined. He looked gorgeous and dangerous...and she felt guilt-ridden and very nervous.

Patrick could hear the hum stretching from her to him. Though she stood in the shadows and he couldn't see her eyes, he could feel them on him. Her nervousness was a tangible thing. That was something he decided to take care of immediately. She was his now, and the unorthodox circumstances that had brought them together no longer mattered. They were married, and he'd never been half-committed to anything in his life.

He reached into the shadows and pulled her to him. "Relax," he chided quietly, holding her loosely in the circle of his arms. "The hard part's over. We've done the deal. All we have to do now is pretend fate brought us together rather than convenience. As though our eyes met across a crowded room."

It would have to be her secret that that was precisely how she felt about their relationship.

"It's just..." she said softly, aware of his thigh against hers, her breasts a hairbreadth from his chest, "that . . . doing the deal . . . is scarier than planning it was."

"You've read my file," he said, brushing a wave of thick dark hair out of her face. "Sin assured you I'm a nice guy." He grinned and she smiled. Then he added lightly, "All you have to do is be completely obedient and we'll get along beautifully."

Her smile became a laugh. "Because I *have* read your file, I know you're not teasing." She looked up into his eyes. "I'm sure from what my father's told you about me, you know that's a futile hope."

He didn't seem concerned. "We'll see. I can be pretty persuasive."

"Marine charm backed by a missile launcher?"

He shook his head, saying softly, "I have my own arsenal." And then he opened his mouth over hers again as he'd done on the lawn. That kiss had been meant to alarm her. This one had a coaxing, taunting purpose, and he used it with the skill of a master.

Her whole body tensed, though all he touched was the tip of his tongue to the inside of her mouth. He explored lightly, playfully, and she found herself leaning into him until her mouth was exploring his.

Then she felt his hand flatten against her back and draw her closer. She gasped and he swallowed the sound as he wrapped her tightly against him and took the kiss higher, deeper, farther than she'd thought a kiss could go. She lost awareness of everything but his roving hand and the beat of her body, rising and quickening.

Then he drew away and gave her a quick, punctuating kiss. She took a step back, annoyed, as she interpreted the point of the lesson.

"You want me to see what I'll be missing if I don't cooperate?"

He held the point of her chin between his thumb and forefinger and studied her face slowly, lingeringly, as though something there read very clearly.

"No," he said, pinching her chin, "I want you to know what you'll gain if you do. Ready to get something to eat?"

HE MADE HER PICK the restaurant, ordered everything she asked for down to the green-tea ice cream with almond cookies, and talked honestly about the hotel and what he intended to do with it. She had difficulty sustaining her annoyance. In fact, he was being so agreeable she began to have renewed confidence in her cleverness in selecting him.

"Tell me about Sin," she said when the waitress took their plates away and they sat over a fresh pot of tea. "How did you meet?"

"In school," he replied, the tips of his large fingers turning the tiny handleless Chinese cup. "We were roommates in the dorm at the University of Puget Sound." He laughed, still staring into the tea. "Hated each other on sight. I took him for a society snob and he thought I was a country rube. Then I explained the theory of relativity—or what we know of it—to him, and he backed me up in a brawl in the cafeteria. We've been friends ever since."

"A brawl over what?" she asked.

"What else? A woman, or in this case a nineteen-year-old cheerleader I had just dated that some jerk tried to tell me was..." He hesitated, choosing his words.

Gina smiled, charmed that he edited his language because of her presence. Men seldom did that anymore.

"I understand," Gina said. "Was she?"

"Yes."

"But not with you?"

"I hadn't asked her." He sipped his tea and grinned. "I *was* a rube. Anyway, getting back to Sin, he always had money and I always had a place to go to on holidays."

"Is Sin orphaned?"

Patrick shook his head. "Abandoned, but not orphaned. His father runs a powerful international law firm, and his mother's from an old family in Philadelphia. He globe hops and she raises money for all the important causes."

Gina nodded sympathetically. "I can relate to that. It's hard to be the last thing on your parents' mind."

"I think your father cares for you," Patrick said. "He's gone to a lot of trouble to find you a husband."

"Mostly he didn't want an indiscreet daughter to turn him into another press powder keg." She toasted Patrick with her cup. "So he called in the marines."

Some subtle change was taking place in her. He didn't know what had precipitated it or where it was leading, but she was getting edgy.

"I'm a civilian now," he reminded quietly.

She sighed. "And I'm a bride. Isn't life interesting?"

He saw the flash of concern in her eyes and decided to approach it head-on. "Is that what's bothering you? Are you afraid of going to bed with me?"

She held his gaze as she sipped more tea. Then she put the cup down and reminded him quietly, "I'm the one who asked *you* for a baby, remember?"

"You're also the one who said doing the deed is scarier than planning the action."

Also harder on the conscience, she thought. If she told him about the possible danger from the black Mercedes, he could have her back home in a few hours.

If she remained in Los Angeles, the press would continue to haunt her, embarrassing her father as he began his campaign and making her own efforts to reestablish her reputation more difficult.

No. She needed this passport to Oregon and anonymity. But she wasn't going to bed with Patrick until she could explain everything. And she couldn't do it tonight.

"I ... ah ..." She rubbed a stiffening spot between her eyebrows. "I'm not scared, I'm ..." She looked at him candidly. "I'm just not ready yet."

He held her gaze, his own dark and questioning but calm. She was beginning to like that about him.

"My stake in this," he said, "was the money, and I have it. Your risk was to come with me to Oregon. Whether you spend the nights in my bed or not is your call."

Perversely Gina found his tolerance a relief and a disappointment.

"Thank you," she said in a tone that didn't sound grateful.

PATRICK TURNED the truck into the motel parking lot, braking to a stop in front of the office and turning off the motor. "I'll get a second room," he said. "I'll just be a minute."

When he disappeared inside, Gina leapt out of the truck feeling quarrelsome and edgy. She headed for the room they already had, unwilling to examine the reason for her mood.

She found the third door from the end, then groped in her purse for the key Patrick had given her. It didn't fit. She looked at it in consternation, then at the room number. The brass numbers on the door said 200. The painted number on the tab on the key chain was clearly marked with a two and a zero, but the third digit was just a curve at top and bottom; the middle was worn away. Is it 203, she wondered? Or 208?

She walked along the gallery, her irritation temporarily supplanted by concern about finding their room. Gingerly, she tried her key in room 203.

The door flew open. Two men wearing black fezzes with a dagger symbol and silver tassels on them looked back at her. One was short and stout with a cigar in his mouth, the other tall and spare in a T-shirt and dress pants. Both were obviously inebriated.

"Well, aren't you a looker!" The stout man said with a broad wink. "Worth waiting for, after all. Come on in." He grabbed her wrist and tried to tug her into the room.

For an instant she thought they had something to do with Yale or whoever owned the black Mercedes. They'd found her!

"No!" she shouted, pulling frantically against him.

"Honey, this is the right room," the taller man said urgently. "Gus and Billy from Eureka. We sent for you. Armstrong from the Fresno chapter set it up."

Gina glared at him.

"Got your money right here." He held up a spray of twenty-dollar bills.

A corner of Gina's mind was thinking this would make a hilarious story to tell Bobbi. The two inebriated gentlemen had nothing to do with Yale. It was a simple case of mistaken identity. But they were instilling panic in her, anyway.

She was tired and cranky, and her usually clear mind wasn't up at that moment to being mistaken for a hooker by two camel dealers from Eureka.

PATRICK TOPPED the stairs and rounded the corner just in time to catch a glimpse of a slim figure at the other end of the gallery pulling against a meaty hand inside a room.

"No!" he heard her say, her voice high and shaded with fear. "I'm not who you—"

"Now look, little lady," the stout man said around his cigar as he yanked Gina into the room. "We been waiting for you for more than an hour. First you're late and now you're teasing?"

She was now beyond finding anything amusing in the situation. "If you don't let me go," she said slowly, "I'm going to scream for my husband."

The taller man looked pleased. "The 'my husband is just outside the door' game. I like that one!"

But the stout man was looking at her narrowly, trying to push the door closed. "Your husband?"

The door shot back on him with a crash, knocking him onto the foot of a twin bed. "Her husband," Patrick said.

"Patrick!" Gina went to him in blind relief, her annoyance forgotten. He drew her into one arm, his eyes going over the two occupants of the room.

"What's going on?" he asked with ominous quiet.

"It's all right," she said quickly. "It was all a mistake. I misread my key and tried to get into the wrong room. They thought I was…oh, here." She stuffed the roll of twenties into Gus's hand. Or was he Billy?

More than anything else she wanted to get out of that room.

He shook his head in disappointment. "You really aren't . . . ?"

"She isn't," Patrick said quietly, looking from one man to the other. "I could call the police to find her for you." It was a threat rather than a suggestion.

The men looked at each other. The taller one smiled uncomfortably. "We'll wait. Sorry, little lady."

Patrick pushed Gina onto the gallery and closed the door with a slam. He unlocked room 208 and pointed her inside.

She stopped in the middle of the room, torn between laughter and a good cry. All in all, this wasn't the wedding night most girls dreamed about.

He frowned at her, hands on his hips. "You might think twice," he said, "about running off in a strange place among people you don't know."

She sighed. "I wanted to take a shower. I didn't expect to get the wrong room."

"I gave you a key."

She handed it to him. "The number's rubbed off. That's why I tried it on the wrong room."

She expected more condemnation. When he simply tossed the key with his jacket onto the bed and went to the coffeepot in the dressing room, she felt herself relax.

"No Vacancy sign went up while we were at dinner," he said over his shoulder. "You can't have your own room, after all."

Having to share this room was both good and bad news. She wasn't wild about being alone in a room if the Mercedes had followed her. But she also wasn't anxious to have to find a solution to sharing *this* room.

"Want some coffee?" he asked. "You can have first go at the shower while I fix it."

"Please." While she rooted through her bag for her nightgown and robe she tried frantically to think of a sophisticated way to bring up the problem of sleeping arrangements.

"We'll have to share the bed," he said, rather absently she thought, as he filled the carafe with water, then plugged in the cord. "But it's a king. Room for a lot of caution between us." He grinned. "I can be trusted if you can."

His easy dismissal of what had seemed to her an insurmountable problem set her further off balance. She was now sure of what she'd suspected when she'd first seen Patrick Gallagher—she'd never met another man like him.

WELL, he'd thought he could be trusted. Patrick poured coffee into a cup at the dressing-room counter, unable to keep his eyes from the sight reflected in the mirror of Gina walking to the bed. She wore a white silk thing that fell to her ankles and clung like a second, sinuous skin to the swell of her bottom. She bent to fluff her pillow. Coffee spilled onto his hand.

He swore silently and mopped up the mess with paper towels stacked on the corner of the counter. He carried the cup to her and placed it on the bedside table. His eyes fell to the soft ivory flesh disappearing into the white silk, then filling the fabric with a shimmering fullness that threatened to steal his sanity.

"Thank you," she said, warily tugging the blankets up and holding them to her breastbone. "Shower's all yours."

"Right." He handed her the remote control for the television. "I've had my coffee. You can refill with what's left in the pot if you want it."

Then he went into the bathroom, leaned into the shower and turned on the cold water, not bothering with the hot.

FEIGNING SLEEP, Gina saw Patrick through the fringe of her eyelashes as he came out of the bathroom. He wore his underwear rather than pajamas, simple cotton briefs and a V-neck T-shirt. As he flipped off the bathroom light and came toward the bed in the glow from the television, she saw the thin fabric of the shirt strained across a broad expanse of shoulder and chest.

When he picked up the remote and turned to click off the television, she saw the taut muscles of his buttocks move under the briefs, before the room fell to darkness.

She closed her eyes tightly and tried to clear her mind. He was so casual about this. Surely she could be the same. But her heart was thudding.

She felt the mattress take his weight, felt him shift once to get comfortable, then there was silence.

ANOTHER SMOOTH MOVE, Gallagher, Patrick said to himself several hours later when the lights were out and he'd been lying beside his bride for ninety-seven minutes. He knew exactly how long it had been because he was counting. It had kept his mind occupied. No, he considered on second thought—it hadn't.

They'd begun this ordeal on their respective sides of the large bed. Gina had politely said good-night, turned her back on him and turned out the light. Ten minutes later he'd heard her even breathing.

In the last hour, he'd been acutely aware of every inch of progress she'd unconsciously made toward him. Restless, she'd tossed and turned, coming ever closer until seven minutes ago—when she'd burrowed into his side and finally stopped moving.

He hadn't budged, either. He'd been afraid to breathe, afraid the cannoning beat of his heart would wake her.

If it did, he couldn't be held responsible for what might happen. He'd married her, after all. She'd asked him to give her a baby! That implied a willingness, even an eagerness to be made love to.

He closed his eyes tightly and tried to clear his mind, but his body remained a raging frame of awakened testosterone.

Chapter Four

Patrick opened his eyes, stared at the pleated floral drapes and wondered where he was. Before his brain could give him an answer, his body became aware of another cause for confusion.

There was a warm, soft pressure against his back. A small, sleepy sound came from it, then a sinuous stirring against his hip and along his leg. There was a burrowing action against his shoulder blade, then stillness.

He remembered.

He resisted the urge to leap out of bed by reminding himself of all the conditions that attended this union. It was only for a year, she'd promised to stay out of his way, but she wanted him to make a baby with her. What more could a man ask for? Lack of permanence, freedom from restraint and sexual privileges. He was in clover.

However, he'd been a soldier long enough not to trust the obvious. The fact that they hadn't made love last night was proof that all the advantages weren't on his side.

There was a sudden, startled movement behind him and Gina sat up taking the blanket with her. He turned onto his back and looked up at her. Her dark hair was a silky tumble around her shoulders, bare except for the thin straps of a nightgown and the blanket clutched at her breast. Her gray eyes, barely darker than opal, blinked twice then settled on him with wary uncertainty.

He felt a sharp pang of lust coupled with a strange disorientation. Those eyes had talked him into this deal. They drew him, snared him and confused him while curiously keeping him at a distance. He should never have done this. He would live to regret it, he was sure.

But the deal was done, and he had to find a way to live with it. He suppressed a chuckle. Ironic choice of words.

He crossed his hands behind his head on the pillow and smiled. "Good morning, Mrs. Gallagher."

SOMETIME DURING the night he'd tossed aside the shirt. Gina knew he'd look like that without it—muscled, broadly proportioned, nothing lean or wiry about him.

He still had a trace of tan, probably from the months in the Middle East, and a wedge of dark, curling hair swept down his chest, over the jut of ribs to his flat stomach, then disappeared under the blanket.

Clutching the covers with one hand, she raised the other to brush the hair out of her eyes.

"Good morning," she replied, making herself smile. She was taut and nervous despite a good night's sleep.

Somehow, in the light of day, that tough, solid body suggested danger rather than comfort. Still clutching the blanket, she reached to the foot of the bed for the white silk robe that matched her peignoir.

"I like to have first dibs on the bathroom in the morning," she said lightly, hoping to assert herself. She pulled the robe on, then yanked the blanket out from under it when it was tied. She tossed the covers aside and stood, feeling amazing relief at putting the width of the bed between them. "Although I imagine your house has two bathrooms?"

He propped up on an elbow, his lazy dark eyes roving her warm cheeks and knowing, she was sure, what was going on in her mind. "Sorry, just one. It's an old house. But I'll get to that when I can. How long are you going to be?"

"Fifteen minutes," she replied, backing toward the bathroom. "Twenty if my hair doesn't cooperate."

He glanced at his watch, then his eyes lifted to her hair. She knew it probably looked like a broom in a state of apoplexy.

He smiled. "Fifteen. Tie it up in a ponytail or something. I'd like to be on the road by nine."

GINA CHECKED the light on her curling iron. She wouldn't wear her hair in a ponytail for anyone, and she was sure she could curl her hair out here in the bedroom before he was finished in the shower.

Feeling domestic, she straightened the covers on the bed and opened the drapes—and screamed.

Her heart pounded hard enough to choke her. A man was staring at her. He was tall and big, wearing a tweed sport coat a size too small. His eyes were large and blue and bulging, and his wide mouth drooped. He stood about six foot five.

Beside him was a much smaller, thinner man, whose beady dark eyes bored into Gina's, and whose lipless mouth curved into a leering smile. She knew without being told how they'd gotten there—the black Mercedes.

She screamed again and ran to the door to replace the chain lock. But before she could reach it, the door burst inward with a crash and the large man was upon her in an instant. He manacled her throat with one beefy hand and bent her backward over the table. The other man snapped the drapes closed and leaned over the big one's shoulder.

"Where is it?" he asked.

Rapidly losing air and composure, Gina went slack under his hand. Beyond the bathroom door, the shower still drummed loudly. Patrick probably didn't even know she was in trouble.

She wrapped both hands around the meaty wrist at her throat and gasped, "Where's...what?"

"Don't get cute. You know what I mean."

She wished she did. "I don't," she gasped again. "Tell me." Little sparkly things were beginning to float before her eyes.

"Can I choke her, Larry?" the big man asked eagerly, his slack mouth taking on an anticipatory smile. "Can I?"

"Easy, Shrimp," Larry replied, leaning menacingly closer to her near-unconscious form on the table. "It's better when you give these things time."

Then everything erupted. Larry's body flew and Shrimp freed her, straightening up in surprise. Shrimp took a blow full in the face from Patrick's booming fist and wasn't even rocked.

Patrick, barefoot and barechested, hesitated in surprise. Before Shrimp could react, Patrick hit him again.

This time Shrimp blinked and shook his head. He looked at Larry crumpled on the floor, then at Patrick with childlike bad temper. Gina heard Patrick's round oath as he backed away and squared off.

"You hurt Larry," Shrimp accused. "I'm going to hurt you!"

Shrimp advanced on Patrick like Goliath after David, and Gina tried desperately to drag in air and clear her brain. Then she remembered the curling iron.

When Gina reached them, Shrimp had big hands around Patrick's throat, completely oblivious to the blows being delivered to his midsection.

She put the hot curling iron to the back of Shrimp's hand and heard a satisfying sizzle followed immediately by an indignant yelp. Shrimp dropped that hand from Patrick.

As Shrimp shook the offended appendage, Gina applied the curling iron to the other hand with the same result. Now free, Patrick continued to batter at Shrimp. Gina ran around behind them to open the door.

Shrimp's long reach caught Patrick's throat again. This time Gina applied the hot barrel of the curling iron to the side of Shrimp's neck. He roared in pain and backed away, looking like a child surprised by another's unkindness. She advanced on him again. This time Patrick grabbed her wrist and slung her out of the way.

Larry appeared suddenly from behind them, running through the door and shouting for Shrimp to follow him. The big man lumbered after his cohort, seeming more than anxious to leave.

Patrick went to the phone while Gina locked the door. "God," he said, quickly reviewing the instructions taped to the table for a call to the desk. "Beirut wasn't this bad! Hookers and johns one minute, thieves and muggers the next. You okay?"

Gina put a hand down on the phone to break the connection. "I'm fine. Let's just go before Shrimp and Larry come back with reinforcements."

"Who?"

"Shrimp's the big guy." She was wrestling Patrick for the receiver as they spoke. "Larry's the other one. Come on. It's quarter of nine and you wanted to be on the road by nine."

Patrick yanked the receiver from her and held her away with his forearm across her chest from shoulder to shoulder. "Gina, two thugs tried to rob us. We should report it to the management and the police."

"No!" she shouted. "Please, Patrick, let's just go. My bag's already in the truck." When he tried to redial, she added anxiously, "They're not thieves. At least, not the way you think."

He frowned, his complete attention suddenly focused on her. He put the receiver down. "What do you mean? You know those guys?"

"Not exactly."

He replaced the receiver, his frown deepening. He folded his arms over his bare chest. "How exactly?"

She sighed frustratedly and caught one of his arms in both hands. "If I promise to explain in the truck, will you come now? Please?"

HE KNEW IT. A deal too good to be true always was. He flew around the room with her for two or three minutes getting all the rest of their possessions back into their bags and their bags into the truck.

"Can I take a minute to put shoes and socks on?" he asked, sitting on the edge of the bed, prepared to do just that.

"You can do that in the truck," she said, snatching up his striped tube socks and Nike running shoes and leading the way to the door. "I'll drive."

"I'M A VERY competent driver," Gina said cheerfully, going much too fast along a truck route that led to the intersection of Highways 1 and 101. That little fracas had completely relieved her feelings of tension and nervousness, and though she should have been frightened that whoever Shrimp and Larry were working for had trailed her to the motel, she felt exhilarated instead that she and Patrick, together, had escaped them. "And you're very good with your fists," she said, feeling magnanimous. "Larry's probably still wondering what happened."

"Pull over," Patrick said.

"What?" Gina glanced at him as she braked for a truck carrying the famous Salinas Valley artichokes. He had a foot propped against the dashboard while he tied his shoe. His return glance was quiet and scary. Temper simmered under his cool control. "Patrick, we have to put some distance between us and them. We have to..."

He didn't bother to argue. He simply glanced into his side mirror at the traffic behind them, then put a hand on the wheel and turned them off the road and onto a long driveway that led to a group of warehouses.

"Stop," he said.

She braked and turned off the ignition. She turned to him with a judicious expression. "That was a dangerous thing to do. You should never take the wheel from another person."

"When a person lies to you," he said, "you don't usually want to follow where she leads. Now, who the hell were those guys and how do you know them?"

"I don't know them," she corrected, then rested her wrists on the steering wheel and stared through the windshield at the poplars that stood tall and green beyond the warehouses. She admitted reluctantly, "I just know they're after me."

"After you," he repeated, obviously waiting for her to explain.

When she couldn't, she just nodded and confirmed with a clear gray gaze on him, "After me."

He was silent a moment, then asked pithily, "Why?"

She shook her head. "That I don't know."

"Then how do you know they're after you, if you don't know *why* they're after you?"

"Because someone's been calling me and not saying anything. Because a black Mercedes has been following me for about a month. I had no idea who was in it until this morning."

He made a sound of impatience. "Did you call the police?"

She turned to him, her expression telling him she knew a little more about this than he did. "Yes. You know how everyone responds to nuisance phone calls?

As though the one complaining is the problem. No one can do anything about it. You should hear what they have to say about my being followed by a black car that shows up in the damnedest places at the oddest times. Then they tell me they read all about me in the paper. That I'm the one who stole the Ming, the Renoir and the diamond necklace. They suggest that I'm delusional.''

Patrick saw genuine distress in her eyes. He didn't want it to complicate his anger. ''Surely your father has some connections that would help you out.''

She studied her hands. ''I haven't told him.'' When he responded impatiently, she said loudly, ''Well, he wouldn't want to hear it. Trust me on that. He's about to launch a campaign, remember? The last thing he'd want is trouble from the daughter who's always embarrassing him.''

Patrick remembered his conversation with Wyatt Raleigh. She was probably right.

She sighed. ''No, this is something I have to do myself. I just want to get away from them until they realize they have the wrong person. Or that I don't have what they think I have.''

He stared at her for a moment without reaction, then he said, as though he finally understood the bottom line on this unconventional deal, ''And I was your way out!''

He pushed his door open and stepped out of the truck. Sure he meant to abandon her, Gina followed, running to catch up with him as his long stride ate up the asphalt drive.

"Where are you going?" She reached a hand out, intending to pull him to a stop, but the look he gave her forced her to reconsider.

"For a walk," he replied.

"Now?"

"Either I walk off energy..." he said, a muscle ticking in his jaw, "or tomorrow morning they find your body in a Dumpster."

She continued to run along with him. "Look, Patrick, I know I didn't handle this the right way, but I..."

He had stopped so quickly, she was three steps ahead of him and still talking before she realized he was no longer beside her. She backtracked warily. His expression could have carved stone.

When she stood in front of him, he said gravely, "You lied to me. You and your father intended to use me."

"No," she denied. "I told you my father didn't know. He genuinely wanted to find me a husband he knew would take care of me, at least until my inheritance comes through. He trusted you. He didn't use you. And, anyway..." Guilt weighed heavily on her, but she folded her arms and looked back at him intrepidly. "You got half a million dollars."

"Like money and honesty are comparable." His expression made her lower her eyes, but only for a moment.

She put the shame she felt behind her, because she had to make him understand. She had to get to somewhere safe until her grandmother's money allowed her to start over. "It's a lot of money, Patrick. My father's a bold investor, but he's not stupid. Had I told you I needed a bodyguard to get me out of town and keep me safe, you'd have refused to marry me. When you did, my father probably would have turned you down. Where would honesty have gotten your precious Candle Bay Inn then?"

She had a point, and much as he hated to, he was forced to examine it. If it hadn't been for the check from Wyatt Raleigh, almost a century of Gallagher sweat and tears would have disintegrated into chapter eleven.

"All I did," she said, pressing her point with a cautious smile, "was save you from yourself. Now that you've got your money, you can keep the renovations going on the hotel and secure the season, and I'll help you start the best child-care facility any hotel ever had. All you have to do in return is keep the goons away from me."

He put his hands in his pockets and leaned his weight on his right foot. "I have the money," he said evenly. "I don't lose a thing if I let them have you."

She felt herself pale but answered quietly, "You'd lose peace with yourself, and for a man like you, that's a lot. You wouldn't do that."

He laughed ironically. "You overestimate my nobility, Gina."

She shook her head. "I don't think so. I read your file, remember? Winner of the Bronze Star, for conspicuous courage."

He started to walk again.

"You took a vow," Gina reminded him as she ran beside him, pressing her advantage. "We're married. You can't just leave me. It wouldn't be right."

"Right?" He stopped again and caught her arm, his dark eyes boring into her cloudy gray gaze. "As though you would know anything about what's right. You set me up, lied to me and played the role of lost little waif like a Hollywood veteran."

She raised an eyebrow. "Lost little waif?" That wasn't the way she'd seen her performance.

He studied her a moment, as though perplexed. "It was in your eyes," he said absently. "This kind of... need."

His gaze was so deep and dark that for a moment she lost herself in it. She lost connection with their surroundings, with the situation, with everything else but the gold flecks in the brown irises of his eyes.

Then he blinked once, straightened and squared his shoulders. She was forced to readjust to the here and now.

"You're telling me," he asked with cool distance, "that you have no idea why those guys are after you?"

"I have a theory," she said, almost reluctant to share it. "But it doesn't make sense."

"What about you does? Let's have it."

"Well, they may have been hired by Yale Gardner, my former partner."

"Why?"

"I don't know."

He shifted his weight again, studied the distance a moment, then looked back at her. "You call that a theory? Theory is usually supported by reason. And, anyway, your father told me Gardner cleaned out your inventory and your bank account and took off for parts unknown."

She nodded grimly. "He did. But I don't know how else to explain it. I have no other enemies."

He laughed mirthlessly, turning back toward the truck at a reasonable pace. "Somehow I find that hard to believe."

She turned with him. "You'll see for yourself. I'm really a very nice person." When he slanted her a doubtful glance, she returned a smile. "I'll make all this worth your while. I may have tricked you into this deal, but I'll keep my part of the bargain. When I'm not being chased by hoods, I'm an honest human being. I'm even fun to be with."

"Apparently the conventioneers last night thought so, too."

"That was a simple misunderstanding."

"That was an indicator of things to come. You're trouble, Gina Raleigh, and I already have all the trouble I need."

She stopped beside the truck and turned to face him. "I *am* trouble," she said. "My father's always said so.

I attract it, even when I'm minding my own business. It's a fact I can't help. But you'd only have to put up with it for eleven months.'' She paused and lifted her chin. ''And my name is Gina *Gallagher*.''

Patrick looked down at her, hands on his hips, waiting for his usually dependable brain to come up with a solution to the dilemma. But all he saw was a very pretty girl who now bore his name and still had that lost look in her eyes. Could it really be that the need in her was honest even if the woman wasn't?

If that were true, he couldn't in all conscience let himself off the hook. But he wasn't letting her off, either.

With a swift movement Gina hadn't seen coming, he grabbed her arm and backed her up against the truck door, planting a hand on the steel on either side of her head. Though her instinct was to flinch, she made herself look him in the eye as he leaned over her.

''There's implied honesty in all contracts, you know,'' he said with quiet intensity. ''By rights, even a noble man can walk away from a contract in which he's been deceived.''

That would be the end of everything. Gina swallowed. ''In this case,'' she said, thinking fast and dangerously, ''the noble man would be a foolish one. If you walk away now...'' She hesitated, dropped her eyelashes significantly, then looked up at him with wide gray eyes and went on in an undertone, ''You'll never know what you missed.''

Long years of conditioned control prevented him from reacting to her suggestion. Everything he'd felt that morning when he'd awakened with her curled against his back came back to haunt him. He was beginning to wonder if half a million dollars would ever be worth the frustration.

"Please," he said dryly. "You needed more time, remember?"

She heaved a little sigh that he felt against his chin and said softly, "Tonight could be a new beginning. But not if you walk away."

His mind was made up.

"Oh, I don't intend to walk away." His eyes darkened when he saw hers flare with victory. She noted that subtle reaction and subsided when he moved even closer. "I'm going to get every last point of the contract that's coming to me, but if you lie to me again, we're history and you're on your own. Is that clear?"

She nodded, lowering her lashes this time so that the glow of success didn't show. "You just have to put up with me for eleven months," she said, finally looking up at him again, her expression serene, "and I'll walk out of your life. Hopefully, pregnant."

He frowned. "I said no baby."

"I heard you."

Patrick studied her calmly innocent expression and knew handling this woman was going to require every tactical skill he had. He straightened and lowered his arms. "Get in the truck," he said.

She turned to open the driver's door, but he caught her arm and turned her to the passenger's side. "From now on," he said, "I'm in the driver's seat."

Chapter Five

"You're taking Highway 1?" Gina asked in disapproval as Patrick took the marked turn that led them away from the pastoral stretch of Highway 101 through the Salinas Valley. "Have you ever driven 1?" Gina looked back over her shoulder at the traffic turning onto 101. "It's hours longer. It twists and turns and dips and climbs the Santa Lucia Range to its highest point. They make jokes about it. It's like driving the Alps!"

Patrick nodded, relaxing as the traffic thinned and the sun, now high in the sky, dappled the blue Pacific Ocean. "Sin and I drove it during spring break our senior year in college. The conditions will also make it difficult for whoever's after you to try anything on the highway. We'll have the cliff side. For them to mess with us, they'd have to take the water side and they're probably not that stupid." Then remembering Shrimp, he qualified that by saying, "Well, maybe the skinny guy isn't."

Resigned to her fate, Gina settled in her seat and relaxed. "His name's Larry."

"Right. I forgot you're on a first-name basis."

A sudden, vivid memory of the few moments Shrimp and Larry had had her bent backward over the motel table reminded her that she hadn't thanked Patrick for coming to her aid. "Thanks, by the way."

He set the cruise control and with the road ahead and behind them clear, gazed at the sparkling expanse of water. "For what?"

"A few more seconds with Shrimp's hand around my throat," she replied, "and you'd be a widower."

He glanced her way and smiled. It was the first smile he'd given her that expressed genuine amusement. She felt it warm her like the sun on the water. Until she realized it was probably thoughts of her death that had amused him. "Interesting prospect," he said, turning back to the road. "Have you had time to sign your life insurance over to me?"

She grinned grudgingly. "Sorry. But being a widower would still have its advantages. It would give you a great deal of appeal to young, single women. You could start fresh with some willowy blond thing bent on comforting you and who doesn't attract trouble or want a baby."

"I can do that in a year, anyway," he said. "I guess we'll just do our best to keep you alive."

"WE MISSED BREAKFAST," Patrick said, glancing at his watch. "Want to stop for an early lunch?" He turned briefly to give her a questioning look.

He was being remarkably civil, given the circumstances. She was anxious to cooperate.

"Please," she said with genuine enthusiasm. "I've usually had a full breakfast by now."

"We'll get a sandwich and walk along the beach. Stretch our legs."

He turned off the highway just beyond Cambria.

"Sounds good." She was already feeling stiff and confined.

"The only condition," he said, heading for the road that ran along the water, "is that you stay glued to me. No wandering off."

That condition had an appeal she chose not to consider at the moment. It was easy to agree to.

The small town faced the ocean and was set in a half-moon bay in the shelter of tall, steep bluffs. She gazed longingly at the inviting little shops as Patrick led the way to a fast-food restaurant near the water. When she paused to look into a bookstore window, he caught her hand and tugged her along with him. "No time for that," he said. "We need food, a little exercise, then we've got to get back on the road."

"Right." Her hand was enfolded in his much larger one, her shoulder bumping companionably against his upper arm. *This is nice,* she thought, recognizing candidly that it was far more than she deserved.

THEY ORDERED hamburgers, seasoned fries and colas and carried them to the water's edge where they found a low wall of boulders that stretched out into the ocean. Carrying the white bag that contained lunch, Patrick climbed up nimbly, then pulled her up after him and out onto the finger of rock.

A few feet short of the tip, he found a flat section, eased Gina onto it and folded up beside her. He distributed the contents of the bag while Gina inhaled the wonderful freshness of the breezy waterfront. Her gaze caught the flight of a bird, curiously prehistoric looking with its considerable size and angles. Long bill pointed downward, it made a kamikaze dive toward the water.

Gina pinched Patrick's sleeve between thumb and forefinger and shook it. "Look, a pelican!" She pointed with her other hand, then shaded her eyes with it as the big bird hit water with an awkward splash.

Patrick studied her speculatively as he handed her a straw. He wanted to throttle her after the way she'd tricked him, but some surprising ingenuousness in her kept surfacing and confusing him. "Never seen one?" he asked.

"Of course," she replied, absently tearing the end of the wrapper. "But I just don't get to the beach that often since I sold my place in Santa Monica."

He placed a paper napkin on her bent knee. "I didn't know rich girls got excited about things like pelicans."

"Are you going to pull some reverse snobbery thing on me?" Apparently unconcerned with his answer, she worked on sliding the straw from its wrapper.

He popped a fry into his mouth and shook his head while he chewed. "No. It's just nice to know you appreciate the simple things. For the next year that's all that will be available to you."

She raised a haughty eyebrow. "Maybe you could let me look through a Tiffany's catalog once in a while to keep me focused on what you think I consider important."

"Don't be snide," he admonished.

"Then don't assume you know me when you don't," she returned. "Did you get ketchup?"

He peered into the bag. "Nope. They're seasoned fries. They don't need ketchup."

"I always need ketchup."

"Try to manage without. Practice austerity for the year ahead."

He was surprised an instant later when a soft, harmless missile hit him in the face. He disentangled Gina's straw wrapper from his burger and balled it in his fingers, giving her a threatening look.

She contemplated a french fry. "I thought a soldier would have been better prepared for attack. Goes to show you. People aren't always what they seem."

He tossed the wrapper into the empty bag, thinking she was more trouble than he'd imagined she would be, but more interesting also. "You," he said, "appear to be trouble, and you are. It's been my experience—" he put the paper bowl of fries he held aside and dusted off his hands "—that those who initiate a conflict are seldom prepared for the counterattack."

In a move she never saw coming, he pushed her backward on the rock, cushioning her head in his hand. He leaned over her, grinning into her wide gray eyes. "They leave themselves vulnerable to the enemy."

She felt small and helpless as the vastness of the sky seemed to recede even farther beyond his head. He was always trying to frighten her, she thought. Always trying to keep her intimidated and at a distance.

She met his gaze intrepidly, though her voice was breathless. "I don't think of you as the enemy."

He studied her a moment with a mild frown, then straightened and pulled her back to a sitting position. "Maybe you should."

"You didn't leave me alone in this. You stayed with me. An enemy wouldn't do that. Thank you."

The need in her eyes was overlaid by a sweet, genuine gratitude. He had difficulty holding out against it, but he wasn't about to be fooled a second time. "Assuming you mean that, you're welcome. Whether you do or whether you don't, you're going to have to be the ideal wife to guarantee my continued support."

Her face fell, hurt feelings sharp in her gray eyes. She got to her feet, her slim body in stirrup pants and a long white sweater silhouetted against the cloudless blue sky and the sparkling ocean. She opened her mouth to speak, then changed her mind and moved as far away from him on the rock as she could get and sat down and ate her lunch.

When she'd finished, she stood to leave, pretending he wasn't there.

Her progress was arrested immediately by the long leap required from their flat dining rock to the next one with enough surface to land on.

Patrick got to his feet, balled their bag of trash into the palm of one hand and made the leap. Then he turned to offer her a hand. She leapt, colliding with his chest on the scant surface of the rock. For a minute he held her there, her breasts against his chest, the lower part of her body pressed against him by the hand that anchored her in place. Everything inside her fluttered and beat.

Patrick felt the impression of her breasts against his ribs and her thigh between his. It incapacitated him for a moment. That gave him time to become aware of the floral scent of her hair, of the fragility of the frame he held to him with one hand, of the nervous flutter of thick, dark eyelashes. He had the sensation of having been caught by one of the sirens of legend whose cries lured men onto the rocks to their death.

Without taking time to consider the wisdom of the move, he lowered his mouth to hers. It was soft, cool and salty from the coastal breeze, and open in surprise. He took swift advantage.

He coaxed her lips into compliance, then teased her with his tongue, losing some of the frustration he'd felt during their long night without touching in the king-size bed. She responded with an eagerness that surprised him. He took a fistful of the back of her hair and delved deeper with his tongue, needing to show her that he would be tolerant, but he would be possessive and demanding also.

Gina was surprised and delighted with his ardent kiss. She felt all the complications between them fade into the background until only holding him and being held mattered. She gave herself over to the comfort and excitement, feeling a kind of blessed rightness in his claiming touch.

"I WONDER," Gina said quietly, reverently, "if anyone would grow accustomed to the beauty of Big Sur? I mean, if you lived here and saw it every day?"

She had unbuckled her seat belt and was straining sideways to see beyond Patrick to the surf thundering against the cliffs. He glanced down to see the eerie mist created that made everything look like a page from prehistory.

Flanking the right side of the highway was a primordial mountain forest that was home to the southernmost stands of coast redwoods.

"The type of person who'd want to live here," Patrick replied, "is probably not the type of person who'd ever fail to notice his surroundings, no matter how familiar they became."

"Look," she exclaimed. "Mailboxes."

His eyes followed her pointing finger to a wooden benchlike affair that held more than a score of rural mailboxes.

She looked around, ducking down to look higher up, turning to look over her shoulder. "I wonder where the homes are. I don't see anything resembling a structure."

"I don't imagine someone would choose to live here and then build right on the highway." Patrick guided the humming truck steadily along the curving road. "They're probably back in the folds of the mountains somewhere."

Gina settled back in her seat. "You think you have these people all figured out, don't you?" she asked. "Just like you think you understand me."

"You asked about where they live," he replied easily. "It's my job to know what people want in the way of shelter."

She allowed him that. It made sense.

She put on her seat belt and leaned back, now watching the rich green on her side of the road.

"I wonder if there's a Bigfoot in there?" she asked. She rolled her head along the headrest to look at his profile. It was gorgeous, she noted. "Do you believe in creatures trapped in time, in things that can't be explained?"

He tossed her an indulgent glance and turned back to the road. "I believe in everything that I don't know for certain to be false. Do you believe in ever being quiet?"

She laughed softly. "I feel dozy, so I won't be talking for a while. Wake me if you lose your way or need a tire changed or something."

Patrick glanced at her, then smiled to himself as she curled up in her seat as much as the seat belt would allow and closed her eyes.

GINA WOKE to busy, tree-shaded city streets. Old Spanish architecture rubbed shoulders with modern glass and stone amid a landscape lush with greenery.

"Monterey," she said, rolling her window down to get a closer look as Patrick stopped at a light. "Isn't it wonderful? If things go well with us," she teased, "I think we should have a summer home here." She turned to grin at him. "What do you think?"

His grim expression surprised her. What had she done now?

"I think," he said, glancing into the rearview mirror, "that you should close your window and get down in your seat. Now."

She didn't have to ask why. "The black Mercedes."

"Well, *a* black Mercedes. About four cars back. I don't know if it's *the* Mercedes, but we'll find out. I'm going to look for a turn sheltered by trees or bushes. If it's your friends, they'll be watching for me to do it, and they'll be right on us. If it isn't, we'll just find a gas station and catch our breath."

"I vote for the second choice," she said.

"Yeah." He pushed her head down a little farther as the light turned green. "Me, too."

Gina stared at the floor mats as Patrick proceeded with the traffic.

"Turn coming up," he warned quietly. "Hold on."

He flipped the signal on, took the left turn at normal speed, then took another sharp left, nosing the truck into a high hedge that marked the border of a park. He braked, put a hand on Gina's head to keep her down, then leaned over the steering wheel to wait.

A spiffy blue Dodge Shadow crossed the intersection and kept going, followed by a battered yellow Toyota truck, a bronze Cadillac convertible, and a black Mercedes. From this vantage point, Patrick could see that the driver was a woman and that there was a child's seat on the passenger's side.

He straightened with a sigh and let Gina up. "False alarm. Sorry."

Gina sat up and smoothed her hair, sending him a wry smile as her pulse relaxed. "That's the kind of disappointment I can live with." She pointed across the street. "There's a gas station. Chevron okay?"

He turned the key in the ignition. "Fine."

She sounded relieved. "Good. I can see the candy machine from here."

AFTER PAYING the attendant and washing his hands, Patrick found Gina standing on the cement base of the chain-link fence that ran around the station. She was staring at the ocean about half a block away and at a row of gnarled cypresses that stood on a bluff overlooking it. As he watched, she took a bite of a chunky candy bar.

A little annoyed that she hadn't stayed by the truck as he'd asked her, he came up quietly behind her, waited until he saw her swallow, then snaked his arm around her waist, sweeping her from her perch. She uttered a little cry of surprise and kicked furiously. The candy bar went straight up in the air.

He held her against his side for a moment, squeezing her slender waist punitively. "If I were Shrimp or Larry," he said, "you'd be in the trunk of a black Mercedes right now."

"If you were Shrimp or Larry," she said, pink cheeked and breathless, "I'd have screamed for Patrick."

"You might not have had time to scream."

"Then I'd have bitten or scratched." Still dangling from his grip, she looked slightly backward at him and said gravely, "But I knew it was you."

He looked doubtful. "How?"

"I don't know," she admitted. "I just did."

"You struggled."

"I was surprised when you grabbed me, but I knew it was you."

He put her on her feet, apparently unwilling to argue further. "Next time do as you're told. Let's get moving."

Gina refused to look repentant as he put her into the truck. She *had* known he was behind her. It was as though a light had gone on inside her, as though some so-far-unrecognized radar connected them. The notion was unsettling.

"It's about an hour to Santa Cruz," he said, turning into the traffic. "We'll stay overnight there."

"Sounds good. I'm getting hungry."

He shook his head at her. "You just ate a candy bar."

"Two bites of a candy bar," she corrected. "Thanks to you I lost the rest of it. You owe me a large and wonderful dinner."

He cast her a glance as the traffic began to trace the crescent of Monterey Bay. It held challenge and warning and the suggestion of something else she couldn't quite define.

"I'll see that you get everything you deserve," he said wickedly. "I promise."

"I WAS HOPING for something with a sauna and a pool," Gina said as Patrick pulled into the driveway of a very small motel just outside of Santa Cruz.

"This is better," Patrick said, stopping in front of the office door. "You can't see the parking lot from the road, so they won't spot our truck unless they check every motel lot along the highway."

"Maybe they didn't follow us. Wouldn't we have seen them by now?"

"I don't know. Better safe than sorry. Come on in with me."

Moments later Patrick drove the car around the back of the simple structure that housed twenty units, ten on each of two levels. "Another advantage to this place," he said, parking in front of room 107, "is that there's only one wing. Impossible for you to get lost."

"Very funny."

"The restaurant looks good," he said, indicating the neon sign depicting a squatty little chef wielding a fry pan. Plaid curtains were visible from the windows, and a cozy glow of light promised atmosphere. He took her chin between his thumb and forefinger and gave it a playful pinch. "Maybe they'll have a big steak for you, a rack of ribs, a plump chicken and an all-you-can-eat salad bar. Will that keep you till breakfast?"

"If I don't have to work too hard," she said.

She got out of the truck and reached into the back for her makeup case and his tote bag. She handed him his bag with a grin. "Better carry your own so I can save myself." He took their large bags from the truck and unlocked the door to the room.

It was less Spartan than the outside suggested. The shower boasted a hand-held spray that went a little way toward making up for the lack of a sauna. They showered, changed clothes and headed for the restaurant.

"TELL ME ABOUT Gardner," Patrick said before they'd eaten dinner.

Gina looked first surprised, then grateful for a new focus of attention.

She sipped at her coffee and frowned, wondering how she'd come to this point when she and Yale had shared friendship and professional dedication only months before.

It wasn't hard to remember the curious chain of events, though she'd tried to make a point of putting it out of her mind. The press hadn't let her.

"Your father told me you'd met in school," Patrick said, thanking the waitress with a nod as she placed a coffee nudge in front of him.

Gina was momentarily distracted by the generous dollop of whipped cream on top of it.

"I gathered he wasn't in favor of your partnership."

She had to smile. "That's true. But I couldn't look upon Dad's disapproval as any kind of sign that I was making a mistake. He disapproves of me on principle because I don't revere money and position as he does. I think I'm a throwback to my maternal grandmother who turned her back on the family fortune and ran off with a trumpet player."

"What about Gardner?"

Gina shrugged, still surprised that what had looked so perfect had blown up in her face. "He'd been in my art history class. We met again after school at a party. We'd both been thinking about getting into the decorating business, but he didn't have enough capital and I wasn't sure I had the business sense to make it work." She smiled, reminiscing. "We talked about it after the party over a drink and decided we were the perfect business partnership.'' She had difficulty keeping her eyes off the whipped cream slowly dissolving in its pool of boozy coffee.

''No romance involved?'' he asked. Then he noticed her greedy gaze. ''You want a nudge of your own?''

She shook her head in answer to his first question. ''Just friendship and business.'' To his second, she smiled winningly. ''I don't like alcohol in my coffee, but I do have a thing for whipped cream.'' She looked at it anxiously. It was already seeping into the brew, marbling and lightening the coffee color.

Patrick dipped his spoon into it, captured a fat, curly blob and reached across the table to put the spoon to Gina's mouth.

She took the cream, feeling its coolness on the heat of the spoon as he drew it slowly back. The cream dissolved instantly on her tongue, but the look he gave her lasted into her dreams.

''What went wrong between you?'' Patrick asked quietly.

''Simple thievery, I think.'' Gina tossed her head, having to take another sip of coffee to stabilize her pulse. ''We worked together beautifully for almost two years. Our clients were more than pleased with our work, they told their friends, and our base was growing at a rate that surprised even me.'' She sighed, put her spoon down and took another sip of water.

''Then about three months ago a client called to tell me that a Ming vase was missing from the bookshelf

in her husband's home office. Because we'd just re-
done the room for her and had a fireplace put in, I assumed she suspected the mason. I told her we knew
him to be more than honest and completely reliable,
that we'd used him countless times before. She considered us responsible because our firm had been in
possession of her house key for the six weeks it took
to finish the job.''

''So you had to make good?''

''We're bonded. It was a relatively simple matter,
but the same thing happened again three weeks later.
This time it was a Renoir missing from the bedroom
of a friend of my father's. Daddy almost had a
stroke.''

''You'd just finished a job there, too?''

''Two months earlier. Immediately after that it was
a diamond necklace. I didn't want to believe the scenario that was beginning to form in my mind. Someone was copying the keys clients gave us and using
them to steal antiques and valuable artifacts. And I
knew it wasn't me.''

''You confronted Gardner.''

''I tried. He was supposed to be working on the
soap star Susie Burns's winter home in Palm Springs.
I called to talk to him and was told by the maid that
he'd never arrived. She just assumed Burns had called
us to change plans.'' She sighed, her mood grimly ac-
cepting as she recalled what happened next.

''I went to his place and found it locked up tight.
But there was enough of a chink in the draperies to tell

me he'd moved out. Everything was gone. I went immediately to a warehouse we kept near the shop and found that he'd cleaned it out. And that included pieces of furniture we were refinishing or reupholstering for clients. The next morning I discovered he'd cleaned out our business account, also. By that point I wasn't even surprised.''

''What'd you do?''

''The only thing I could do. I called the police and began to liquidate. My place at Malibu had to go, along with my Carrera, and a few pieces of good jewelry I had. But I won't be completely out of debt until I come into my inheritance from Grandmother.'' She held her cup up as the waitress came by with the coffeepot. ''The worst part is that I can't believe I could've been so wrong about someone.''

Patrick raised his half-empty nudge and had it refilled. ''Maybe it wasn't something he'd planned. Maybe he was the good friend you thought he was, then got into drugs or gambling or something that made him lose his head and turn to the first available source of salvation. It doesn't excuse him, of course, but it doesn't make you responsible.''

She put her cup aside and leaned an elbow on the table, propping her chin on her hand. ''You know, for a man who makes no bones about liking things his way, you can be very understanding and compassionate. Why is that?''

Momentarily surprised and disarmed by the compliment, he had to think a minute. ''I baby-sat teenage recruits for a lot of years. I guess it's a lot like being big brother or father in a very large family."

"You know," she said thoughtfully, "I'll bet you'd make a good one."

"A good what?"

"Father," she replied. Then she smiled tauntingly. "You're sure you don't want to have a baby with me? I mean, you have to consider it sometime. Who'll take over the Candle Bay Inn when you go to your reward?"

Patrick frowned at Gina as the waitress put their main courses before them. When she took the soup and salad things away, Patrick leaned forward and said quietly, "If it's all the same with you, I'd rather not consider my death at this moment. I figure I still have another fifty years to make the next generation of Gallaghers."

"All right," she said lightly, contemplating an aromatic chicken breast marinara with obvious anticipation. "If you want to take that chance. What with global warming, El Niño, the imminent cataclysmic earthquake, not to mention the ever-present threat of nuclear..."

"Regina." He said her name softly, but with an edge of firmness that silenced her. He was forcing the sternness in his eyes, she knew, because a light of amusement flickered under it.

"Yes?" she asked innocently.

"Enough," he replied. "One more word out of you during dinner and you forgo dessert."

She looked injured. "But they had custard with hard sauce."

He was unmoved. "The decision's yours."

"Militarist."

"Motor mouth."

"COME ON," Patrick said, catching her hand as they left the restaurant. "Fresh air'll do us both some good." There was a break in the light traffic on the highway that bordered the beach, and he pulled her with him as he ran across.

The air was cool and salty. Gina shivered as she drew in a deep breath. In the distance a bright pattern of lights danced into the water.

"I wonder what that is?" she asked, shivering again.

Patrick stopped, pulled off his leather jacket and dropped it onto her shoulders. "According to the brochure I read in the room while you were showering, it's an old-fashioned boardwalk."

The silk lining was warm from his body, the leather pleasantly heavy. When Patrick put an arm around her to hold the jacket in place, Gina leaned into him as though it was the most natural thing in the world.

"I'll bet they have Skee Ball and a Ferris wheel and snow cones," she said dreamily.

"Don't tell me," he teased. "You once wanted to run away with the carnival."

She laughed. "No. I was just wondering what it would be like to take this trip in a relaxed way, without having to look over our shoulders to check the rearview mirror for a black Mercedes.''

As a strong gust of wind blew, Patrick stopped her to help her put her arms in the sleeves of the jacket and snap it closed. The jacket fell to mid-thigh, and her hands were lost halfway up the sleeves.

''Maybe you'll have that opportunity one day. Are you good at Skee Ball?''

''No, but I'm pretty good at the shooting gallery.''

''No kidding. Me, too.''

They walked on, arm in arm, the ruffly fingers of the surf milky white in the darkness. ''Well, of course,'' she teased. ''You have an unfair advantage. You've had training. I'm self-taught.''

''Then we'll have to shoot it out one day,'' he challenged. ''See which approach is better.''

They continued on in silence for a moment, then she said quietly, ''I'm sorry your return home has been delayed by all this. The coast route will take an extra day and a half.''

He dismissed the inconvenience with an inclination of his head. ''It's all right. I like to be on hand, but I'm sure my staff's doing just fine without me.''

All kinds of things she'd had difficulty saying were suddenly easy to admit in the silky darkness. ''I'm also sorry I lied to you.''

He stopped and turned to her. The sincerity in her tone dissolved whatever anger remained over their situation. ''You've already apologized for that.''

She shrugged a shoulder hidden somewhere in the jacket. "I know. I'm just not sure one apology covers it. I...I'll do everything I promised. I'll set up a great child-care center for you. And I'll—you know...I'll try to be helpful and supportive and...I'll..." She stopped on a sigh.

"Make love to me?" he asked, the quiet question still crystal clear despite the busy sounds of the surf. She felt her lungs dispel a gasp of air.

"Yes," she whispered with what little breath she had left.

He looked at her ivory face uplifted to him in the darkness and forgot how this had all begun, forgot that she'd lied to him, and knew only that at that moment he wanted her very much.

But he'd never in his life taken a woman who hadn't wanted him.

A fragrant breeze stirred her hair, and he put a gentle hand to the cold, silky strands to hold them in place. "We'll wait," he said, "until you *want* to make love to me. Not as a condition of a deal, but because you just can't do otherwise."

She caught his arm as he would have led them back the way they'd come. She didn't try to explain it. She didn't understand it herself. But the attraction she'd felt the first day she'd met him had grown steadily since, fueled by his tolerant if not patient handling of the difficult situation.

"I want to," she said.

He heard emphasis on the second word that gave the statement a flattering validity he had to accept.

He swept her up in his arms and started across the sand to the highway.

Her heart pounding, her face burrowed in his throat, Gina felt his warm, strong arms and knew without a doubt how right this was, however it had all begun. She wanted to make love with Patrick even more than she wanted the black Mercedes out of her life.

She heard Patrick's steady footfalls cross the highway, heard the sound of his tread stop as he crossed the grass that bordered the sidewalk, then held fast to his neck as he stopped abruptly, muttering a quick, emphatic expletive.

Then he suddenly dropped her onto her feet and pushed her into the darkened doorway of the office, jarring her languid mood.

She was so momentarily disoriented that she asked without considering the obvious, "What's the matter?"

Wordlessly Patrick pointed to the thin stream of traffic coming off the freeway. The black Mercedes swept past, gleaming like a breathing, threatening entity under the streetlights. It was not driven by a suburban matron with a child seat on the passenger's side. Larry was at the wheel with Shrimp beside him.

Chapter Six

Patrick grabbed her hand and ran toward the truck. He fumbled once with the key, then turned it in the lock and pushed Gina inside. She unlocked the driver's door as he ran around behind. He was backing out of the parking space before his door was closed, turning sharply toward the narrow alley of space between the office and a redwood fence that surrounded the motel.

"We're going to leave our things?" Gina asked as Patrick braked so sharply that only his arm, quickly thrown out to brace her, prevented her from hitting the dash.

"Depends," he said, easing the door open and slipping out. She scooted along the seat to follow him but he gestured her to remain in the truck with a sharp "Stay there!"

Frustrated, she watched him flatten himself against the wall of the office and peer around the edge.

IF LARRY AND SHRIMP made a casual tour of the parking lot, Patrick thought, straining to see in the dark, it might be safe at the motel when they left. If they started checking rooms, he was hitting the road.

He watched as the powerful halogens of the Mercedes lit a large swath of asphalt as the car pulled up and purred in the motel driveway. He heard the bell jingle over the office door.

So, it was not to be a casual perusal of the parking lot. They were asking questions, probably giving a description of his truck.

In a moment the Mercedes pulled into a parking spot, and the hotel manger appeared with a ring of keys, looking concerned.

As Larry and Shrimp got out of the car, the manager led the way to room 107, saying, "I'd have never taken them for hardened criminals." Then he noticed the vacant spot where the truck had been. "They're gone!"

"Professional thieves," Larry said, "don't usually stick around to pay their bills. Let us into the room. Maybe it'll give us a clue to where they're headed."

That did it. A search of their room, however quick, would give him time to get miles ahead of them. Patrick turned to hurry back to the truck. He collided sharply with Gina, who had crept up behind him. She cried out as he stepped on her foot and knocked her backward.

"Shh!" he cautioned, steadying her. But it was too late. Loud voices from the parking lot told him someone had heard them. He pushed Gina toward the truck, stuffed her in through the driver's side, then followed, pulling the door closed and doing zero to sixty out of the alley faster then the five-year-old Chevy should have allowed.

"We *are* going to leave our things," Gina groaned as Patrick roared toward the freeway. Through the rearview mirror he glimpsed the great good fortune of a semi pulling up in front of the motel, blocking the exit from the alley as the driver, probably weary and anxious to put his head down onto a soft pillow, tried to maneuver his big rig into the three spots in front of the office.

In the time it would take Larry to wait it out or turn the Mercedes around and go out the way he'd come in, Patrick knew he could gain precious miles.

"Here's your chance to really come to terms with the simple life, Mrs. Gallagher," he said, taking over the fast lane and burning up the road. The rest of the light traffic ignored him. "You'll be living in jeans and a sweater for the next year. This is a good time to get used to it."

"I wasn't worried about my expensive things," she clarified, putting the visor down and checking the makeup mirror for signs of the black Mercedes. "Why do you always assume my concerns are material? I was thinking about my comfortable shoes and my makeup bag. I left it on the counter in the bathroom."

He cast her a quick glance as he swung back into the right lane and took a concealed position in front of a truck hauling feed. "I apologize for misjudging you," he said, "but we might have let them get ahead of us, which would have given us an advantage if you'd listened to me and stayed in the truck."

That was true. She didn't want to consider it. She folded her arms and stared out the windshield. The soft, seductive mood of only moments ago was left behind as they sped away. "I'm the one they're after. I have a right to know what's going on."

"You turned my life inside out to get me to protect you from Larry or Gardner or whoever. The prudent thing would be to let me *do* it."

"Just don't try to do it by pushing me around."

The temptation to pull over, back her into the corner of the front seat and set her straight once and for all was almost overwhelming. But there wasn't time.

It was difficult to equate the testy woman beside him with the woman who'd only moments ago admitted she wanted him. Frustration frayed his patience and tautened his nerves. Instead of the romantic end to the evening that had looked so hopeful, he was behind the wheel again, racing through the darkness, pursued by more than one black demon.

As Gina fidgeted beside him, anxious and tired and probably as frustrated as he was, he shook off the discontent and made himself concentrate on what he had to do.

"I don't see them," Gina said, still studying the grill of the truck behind reflected in her mirror. "Can you see the other lanes of traffic?"

He glanced up. No sign of the Mercedes. "Why don't you close your eyes and get some rest. I'll wake you if he catches up."

"Want me to drive for a while?" she asked.

He shook his head. "Thanks. I'm fine."

"How far do you intend to go?"

"Past San Francisco," he replied.

"We could lose ourselves *in* San Francisco," she suggested, pushing her mirror up and turning toward him in her seat.

"I'm counting on them thinking that's what we'll do," he said. "While they're looking for us, we can get most of the way to the Oregon border. We'll find somewhere to hide for a few hours on the other side of town, then get an early start and be long gone while they're still combing Chinatown."

"You're sure that'll work?" she asked doubtfully.

"No," he said quietly, "but at the moment it's all the strategy I can put together. Be quiet and let me think."

She rested her head back and closed her eyes, tired and more than willing to leave him in charge. Particularly since nothing seemed to be going the way she'd hoped.

WHEN GINA AWOKE, there were pinpricks of light in the dark distance, and the freeway traffic had thinned even further. Everything they passed along the road was closed. The windows of gas stations and restaurants yawned hollowly, their security lights illuminating emptiness.

Gina suspected it was very, very late. She sat up, cramped and still tired, and looked at the clock on the dash. One thirty-seven.

Patrick glanced at her and gave her a quick smile. "Sleep well? You missed San Francisco completely."

Gina stretched her arms toward the dash and returned his smile. "I trust you stopped for a loaf of sourdough bread?"

"You're not hungry again?"

"Must be the excitement. Any sign of our 'friends'?"

"No. Ah, there's what I've been looking for."

Gina strained her eyes in the darkness for some sign of a motel. She saw nothing but night and the suggestion of the gentle shadowy roll of a hillside. As Patrick turned onto an unpaved road she hadn't even seen until they were on it, she noticed a tall, irregular shape against the faint, cloudy glow of sky.

"How did you see that?" she asked in disbelief.

"My platoon claimed I had nightscope vision."

Gina studied the ancient barn illuminated in the truck's headlights. Time and weather had dried the wood and left gaps between the boards. It had a cupola with a crooked weather vane, a gaping hayloft door and an open front door that hung drunkenly by one hinge.

"What if somebody lives here?" Gina whispered as Patrick nosed the truck into the barn. "What if there's a farmhouse right over the hill?'' In the glow of the headlights he looked around the obviously long-abandoned structure with its piles of boards and hay littering the floor. She saw shadowy corners and asked doubtfully, ''What if some*thing* lives here?''

He reached into the glove compartment for a flashlight, then killed the motor and the headlights. ''You'd probably like me to roast it over an open fire so you can make a sandwich.''

He opened his door and Gina caught his arm, her eyes wide in the periphery of the light he held away from her face. ''I'm serious, Patrick. I don't like rodenty things. I'm not even crazy about chickens and stuff like that.''

''Then stay in the truck and let me look around first.''

''But you'll be out there and I'll be in here.'' She sighed and decided, ''I'm coming. But if you let anything bite me, I'll see that my father cancels the check.''

''Why don't you stay in the truck?'' he suggested wearily. ''Right now you're in more danger of being bitten by me than you are anything else.''

She considered him a moment, then rolled her eyes and made a scornful little sound. He realized with resignation that he hadn't frightened her.

She followed him, holding on to his left hand as the right wielded the flashlight into all four corners and revealed nothing.

Gina sidled closer to him. "There *are* things in there, aren't there?"

"Probably," he said as a little pile in the shadows changed shape. "But if they're smart enough to stay hidden, I'm willing to respect their privacy. How about you?"

"Yes, definitely." She watched as he flashed the light overhead into the loft. "Think we can get up there?" she asked. A ladder leaned against it, but it looked dry and rickety.

"We'll give it a shot." He handed her the flashlight. "Hold this. I've got a blanket in the truck."

He secured the blanket, handed that to her, also, then leaned a hand on the second rung of the ladder and pushed. It snapped in two. He tried a higher rung with the same result.

Gina looked longingly at the quiet security of the loft. "Guess it's the ground-floor suite for us."

Patrick went to the canopy doors. "Not necessarily," he said. He got in, turned the truck and backed it under the loft until the roof provided a step up to it. Then he parked again, climbed lightly onto the hood, then onto the roof. He was easily within reach of the platform.

He beckoned Gina to follow him. Reaching down to relieve her of the light and blanket, he gave her a hand up to the hood, then onto the roof beside him. He tossed up the blanket and handed her the light.

"Hold it," he said, "until I get up there."

She complied, waiting until he'd swung himself onto the platform. Then she handed up the light and waited while he trained it over the loft. Satisfied, he set the light down beside him, then lay down on his stomach and reached for her.

He pulled her full weight up with one arm so that she could get a handhold on the loft. But she was a few inches short. He steadied her and reached for the seat of her pants.

She squealed when he found nothing to grab of the tight leggings but what they contained. With time of the essence in their precarious position, he unceremoniously hooked a hand high up on her thigh and hauled her up.

As his body reacted strongly to that intimate contact, he wondered how in the hell he was going to survive life with Gina with his libido intact.

Gina wondered if she would ever forget the strength of the biceps she'd gripped for dear life. She didn't have to wonder if she would ever forget the hand wrapped around her thigh. She knew she wouldn't. It made her tingle . . . and want him.

She knew she would never forget any of this. It was like being trapped in a fable, lost in a dream. It had all seemed so easy when her father decided to marry her off at a time when she truly needed a man's protection. But like the princess in the tale, she'd brought the brave suitor danger, and for that she was truly sorry.

As they knelt facing each other in several inches of prickly hay, the light pointing away from them, illuminating the floor of the barn and the strange anomaly of a truck in it, she recaptured, as though uninterrupted, the passion she'd felt on the beach at Santa Cruz.

Patrick felt an unsettling sense of destiny as desire, hot and sharp, washed over him again. God, how he wanted this quirky heiress on the run. This wasn't a Frank Capra movie, he tried to tell himself, this was real life.

But there it was. He'd never been one to deny what he felt. And he felt lust. He also believed in calling a spade a spade. It was a lot more than lust. Every time he looked at her now, he felt an ever-growing weakness—not in his knees, but in his heart. He knew he was going to keep her safe no matter what it cost him. And it was going to cost him his sanity—he just knew it.

"You're exhausted," he said, looking into the opalescent eyes devouring his face. His body was clamoring for her, but this wasn't the right time.

"Actually," she said softly, running her hands over his shoulders, the peaked ceiling making her voice echo. "I'm wide-awake." She felt his strong heartbeat, felt it react to her touch.

He stroked her disheveled hair and warned gently, "The Mercedes could be right behind us."

"For now," she said, leaning into him, putting her teeth to the lobe of his ear, "could we just think about what's ahead of us?"

He had to make himself catch her hands and pull them from him. He kissed her knuckles. "Not until I'm sure you're safe."

"But you're with me."

He smiled wryly. "That's the problem. When I'm with you, I tend to lose awareness of everything else. I almost missed the Mercedes in Santa Cruz. I don't want to forget to listen for it until I'm sure we lost them in the dark."

He took her shoulders and pushed her gently back into the hay, then dragged his hands from her. He turned off the flashlight and lay beside her, pulling her into his arms and opening the blanket over them.

She snuggled into him, feeling remarkably comfortable considering the circumstances.

Patrick felt every inch of her in contact with every inch of him and wondered just how much a man could be expected to endure without snapping. He closed his eyes and tried to rest, knowing he wouldn't sleep. He was bone tired but would make himself listen for another thirty minutes. If Larry hadn't tracked them by then, Patrick would be fairly sure he'd eluded him. Then maybe he could do what he really wanted to do with this night.

GINA AWOKE with a start in the darkness.

"Easy," Patrick's voice said gently. "What's the matter?"

"I . . . don't know," she said, feeling the tension all around her as she leaned up on an elbow. Shafts of moonlight streamed through the roof of the barn, making silver stripes in the air. Motes of dust moved in them, giving them life. She was in the fairy tale again.

"I think I heard something," she whispered covertly.

"You did," Patrick replied, the palm of one cool hand finding her cheek unerringly in the darkness. His thumb strummed her cheekbone.

She felt herself go boneless.

"I said your name," he went on, the hand at her face slipping to cup the back of her neck and pull her gently down to him. "Regina," he said again, the low rumble of his voice now at her ear as he tucked her into his arm and leaned over her. "Regina Gallagher. Mine."

She raised both arms to circle his neck, coming sharply, tremblingly to awareness. The danger posed by the Mercedes was gone for the moment. But she wanted him to be aware that he faced a new and different danger.

"This will make you mine, as well," she said, sensation racing along her throat as his index finger traced a line to the V-neck of her sweater.

Patrick's brain told him that a dangerous pit yawned at his feet, but his body was attempting to tune out, listening only to the touch of fingers on the back of his hand. A part of him that was still soldier—that never relinquished control—fought to hold on.

He combed his other hand into her hair and tugged her head back so that he could look into her eyes. They were already lazy and languid.

"One unromantic question," he said, planting a kiss where his finger had stopped. Then he looked into her eyes. "Are you protected?"

She ran a teasing thumb over his bottom lip. "I don't want to be," she whispered.

"Gina . . ."

"Yes, I am," she said.

"You wouldn't fib to me? Again?"

She accepted the suggestion of censure in his question. "No," she replied. "That's no way to start a marriage."

Satisfied, he lay back, bringing her with him, shifting to lie beside her in the pleasantly spiky hay.

Gina felt confidence in his arms, in the artful mouth that teased her lips apart and in the tongue that delved inside. No man had ever made her feel like this before, as though he knew precisely what she wanted and didn't doubt for a moment his ability to give it to her. Body and soul, she gravitated to the security he offered.

Patrick felt her breasts spread against his chest. He drank thirstily from the mouth she opened to him, realizing how long it had been since he'd had the time to indulge his physical self. Something tugged at his consciousness, something suggesting that even now, before it had really begun, there was more than the simply physical here. But he tuned it out. The situation required simplification, not further complication.

He propped himself on an elbow and gathered up the hem of her long sweater. She raised her arms to allow him to pull it over her head. He placed it under her to cushion her against the hay, then turned his attention to the full breasts blooming from smoky gray lace cups. He unhooked the front closure of her bra and stared a moment at her rosy-tipped ivory perfection.

"You're beautiful," he said.

Then he leaned down to kiss her breast, to take one tight pearl into his mouth, then the other.

Gina shifted restlessly, feeling everything inside her tighten and wait. She tugged his sweater up and pulled it off.

Her eyes roamed the formidable proportions of his pecs and shoulders, glowing warmly in the dark. She planted kisses in the mat of dark hair, encountering warmth and washboard muscle.

He slipped her shoes off, peeled the stirrup pants from her, then hooked a finger in the elastic of her gray lace panties and pulled them down, tossing everything aside.

She unbuckled his belt and unfastened the button of his jeans. She raised her head for his kiss, momentarily hesitant.

Her head still cradled in his arm, he kissed her long and lingeringly, his free hand teasing her breasts, bringing sensation to such bright instant life that all thought of hesitation fled.

Drugged by his ministrations, she reached for the zipper of his jeans and pulled it down. Their snug fit required his help for removal, and she finally dropped them and his briefs beside her things.

He pulled her astride his waist, then wrapped his arms around her to pull her down to him. He stroked every inch of her with a touch at once reverent and possessive.

Fire raced under her skin where his fingers moved— over her back, following the curve of her hip, down her thigh to her knee, then up again, tracing slowly up the back of her leg. Then he reached inside her and her growing tension rose to a high, strained pitch.

She was mindless in a minute, unable to move, unable to think, afraid to breathe. Then he was inside her, his hands on her hips guiding her into the velvet rhythm of a perfect universe.

Even as climax broke over her, she shuddered under its impact, Patrick driving her higher and farther, and she thought she'd never known anything like it existed this side of heaven.

It went on and on, ripples of pleasure that broke one after another, assaulting her with sensation so exquisite she held on to Patrick's hands with desperation, afraid of slipping over into insanity.

Patrick held back until she began to breathe more normally, until that delicious, almost ethereal look left her face, then he pulled her down to him and rolled her over. He plunged deeper inside her and let the pleasure take him. Gina wrapped around him, tightening him into their sexual embrace, and he had a clear instant's awareness of having control wrested from him.

He felt her fingernails stroke from his hipbone up to his shoulder, over his buttocks and up his spine, vertebra by vertebra until his nervous system was a tangle of pleasurable impulses and faulty messages. He shuddered with the power of release, temporarily lost in the net of her sweetness, of the scent of her body and the silk of her hair.

When he could form a coherent thought again, he turned so that she was uppermost once again and yanked the blanket back over them. She lay limp atop him, still breathing hard.

After a moment she pushed herself up and crossed her arms on his chest, her eyes still stunned. "That...I don't...we...God!"

"Yes," he agreed with a deep laugh. "That about says it. If your cooking is half as delicious as you are, I just might keep you forever."

She hid her smug smile in his throat, afraid he'd read in her eyes how much she already wanted that.

"If you prove to be as caring and exciting a husband as you are a lover," she said softly, "maybe I'll want to stay."

His chest moved under her as he laughed again. "Looks like we both have our work cut out for us."

As they lay cozily entwined, Gina snuggled even closer. "Do you think we've lost Shrimp and Larry for good?" she asked.

"No." He ran a thumb gently along her arm. "I think they want you, or something you have, very badly."

"But I don't have anything. Yale took everything we had of value as a company when he left." She sighed heavily. "He left some bolts of fabric, a few chairs that had to be repaired, a plant stand, a base, and a lamp. I sold everything except the lamp when I liquidated."

He looked down at her. "Why didn't you sell the lamp?"

"Because it wasn't worth anything. It's just a painted plaster piece—a sort of Renaissance thing of a couple with a picnic basket running together under the shelter of his cloak. Obviously a rainstorm has ruined an afternoon tryst." She smiled and kissed his chin. "Anyway, I've always rather liked it. I found it at a flea market and bought it on impulse, thinking I'd find the right place to use it one day."

He leaned up on an elbow. "Where is it now?"

"In the back of the truck," she said, scrambling up with him as he got to his feet and started the cautious process to roof to hood to barn floor. "But, Patrick, it can't be the lamp. It's plaster. Believe me, I know a little about this stuff. It's not a valuable antique or anything."

He unlocked the canopy and she pulled open the carton in which she'd wrapped the lamp. He raised an eyebrow as she unwrapped the garishly colored base. The cloak was gold, the young woman's skirt and blouse a gypsy red and yellow, and the man wore purple pants and white shirt with billowed sleeves.

Gina ran a hand lovingly over the cloak. "Don't they look happy? As though they've found the middle of their rainbow." She held it to her and told him firmly, "I'm going to repaint it and find a place of prominence in which to put it, so you may as well resign yourself to it. Does your house have a mantel?"

He gave her a look that told her they would argue that later and removed another wrapped piece from the box. It was the tulip-shaped globe that held a flame bulb and fit into one of the hands with which the young man held the cloak.

Patrick turned it in his hand, frowning. "And this is it?"

She held up an old cellophane bag that held the crystal droplets that hung from the globe. "Except for these."

He winced. "Gina, maybe you should have left this at the flea market."

Indignant, she wrapped the base lovingly and replaced it in the box. "It spoke to me. I had to have it."

"What did it say?" he teased. " 'Here I am, Gina. Waste five dollars'?"

She snatched the globe from him, her lips pursed in disapproval. "It said, 'One day you'll find the right man and you'll both be as happy as we are. Until then, you can look at *us*.' " She nestled the globe into the foot of the box, wove the flaps and replaced it in the back of the truck. She dusted her hands off and looked at him with a haughty tilt of her chin. "And I paid fifty. So go ahead and laugh."

But he couldn't. He closed the canopy, then leapt up onto the hood, drawing her after him. When they were back in the loft, he pulled her sweater off, kicked off his jeans and told her in no uncertain terms that for as long as they were together, he would do his damnedest to put the same look in her eyes as the girl in the lamp had.

Chapter Seven

"Come on. Gina, come on. Look alive." Patrick tugged at the arm Gina refused to put through the sleeve of her sweater. She was slumped sleepily against him, her eyes closed again.

"No," she grumbled as he reached into the cuff of her sweater, caught her fingertips and pulled them through. "It's still dark."

"That's because your eyes are closed," he said, now struggling with the other arm. "Open them. It's dawn. We've got to get on the road."

She smiled, her eyes still tightly closed. "Can't we stay here? Make love again?" As he tugged the sweater down she went on. "Why don't we just move here? I could redecorate. You could sell insurance or something."

"Gina, wake up," he said, sitting her up and patting her cheek until she finally looked at him. "There's nothing to eat within miles of here," he added gravely. "And you haven't had a bite since seven last night."

Gina's eyes widened and she came to sudden awareness. "Oh, my God."

"I thought that'd bring you around."

She stretched her cramped muscles. "I don't want to wear the same things again," she grumbled moodily.

"Lady Godiva had a horse, honey," he said as he swung her off the hood of the truck. "Not a Chevy. When we have time and opportunity, we'll get you a change of clothes."

"And makeup. I need makeup."

He looked at her pink-cheeked, sleepy-eyed face and couldn't imagine paint improving it. But she needed to be humored this morning. "Sure. Whatever."

In a moment she was opening the barn door and Patrick was driving out into the gray early morning.

The road climbed and wound and seemed to go on forever, reaching for the slow-rising misty sun. Like a ribbon the road undulated along a coastline of chiseled rock capped by a carpet of green.

On the land side of the road were tidy little farms where holstein cows grazed lazily.

A little farther, on the water side, they passed long, railed piers with small, brightly painted structures at the end of them.

"I love the privacy," Gina said, pointing to them, "but the places are a little small."

Patrick laughed. "I think they're boathouses. We have one at the inn, but it's a little bigger than those."

"Your guests go boating?"

"Fishing. Best salmon in the world at the mouth of the Columbia River. Have you ever fished?" He grinned and added before she could answer, "Or can you be quiet that long?"

She made a face at him. "No, I've never fished. Have you ever been antique hunting?"

"Can't say I have."

"I'll be happy to introduce you to the experience." When he looked doubtful, she added brightly, "You'd enjoy it. I'm usually very serious and very quiet when I'm antique shopping."

"Then by all means, we'll try it."

"Patrick, I'm starving," she said plaintively. "One more minute without breakfast and I'm going to faint dead away."

"I was hoping we'd have found a restaurant by now." He reached across her to open the glove compartment. A bag of cheddar-and-onion potato chips fell out onto her lap.

"Oh!" she exclaimed as though it were pâté on crackers. "You've been holding out on me."

"I bought them last night when I stopped for gas while you were asleep." He gave her a teasing but indulgent glance. "I had a feeling an emergency would arise."

She tore the top off, dipped a hand in for a chip and chewed, her eyes closed in ecstasy. Then she removed a chip and held it to his lips. He snapped it with a nod of thanks.

"There's also a box of juice in there," he said.

"You're kidding!" She investigated the glove compartment and pulled out an apple juice with a small straw attached to the side. "Patrick, this is ambrosial. You're turning out to be prime husband material. Competent, resourceful, thoughtful."

Then she remembered last night and decided neither of those words described the tender power of his lovemaking. She glanced at him and found him looking at her, a smoky expression in his eyes telling her he was remembering also. It was the first thought they'd really shared, the first momentous experience on which they could look back together from the same perspective.

For the first time since she'd repeated her vows, Gina felt like a wife.

Patrick watched color fill her cheeks, watched her meet his eyes without apology or excuse or regret and felt fiercely and protectively like a husband.

"Competent?" he asked with a dry grin, stretching a hand out to take hers.

She brought his knuckles to her lips. "Last night was magical. You know it was." She sighed, then freed his hand as they came to a series of curves. She had to contend with a completely new impression of him—a passion beyond anything she'd imagined and a tenderness she could still feel in the light of day.

He concentrated on the road, but a corner of his mind that insisted on reliving those delicious hours in the hayloft told him in no uncertain terms that something had changed last night. He'd discovered a generosity in her that surprised him, and a sweetness that left him feeling drugged. He didn't like the uneven feeling, but the memories were too delicious to dismiss.

They found a small roadside restaurant in a little town just north of Fort Ross, a remnant of Russian presence and seal hunting in the nineteenth century.

"Two hamburgers," Patrick said in wonder as he headed north yet again. "I've never seen a woman eat two hamburgers."

She'd brought the rest of her fries with her and shook her head without remorse as she chewed. "One of them was a chickenburger," she said. "They're lighter. Want a french fry?"

"I should be entitled to one," he said. "They were mine after all, but, hey, who would dare stand in the way of..." He lowered his voice and intoned dramatically, "The Woman Who Ate the World."

"I'm trying to keep my strength up," she said, her side-glance righteous. "If we have to run for it or something, I wouldn't want to fall behind."

He gave her a half laughing, half serious glance. "I'd never leave you," he said.

Silence pulsed for one instant, then she asked softly, "Because I'm your wife?"

He stared at the road. "Because you're wearing the only jacket we have between us."

She battled with hurt feelings and disappointment for as long as it took him to lose the straight face. Then she hit him viciously in the upper arm.

He fended her off, reminding her laughingly that this was not a road that would forgive divided attention. Then he patted the middle seat.

"Move over here," he said, reaching behind himself to hand her one end of the belt.

As she buckled the seat belt and settled in next to him, hip to hip and thigh to thigh, she felt a shudder of excitement and a glow of warmth that made her forget this wasn't a real honeymoon.

Patrick rested his arm across her and cupped her knee in his hand. She rubbed her cheek on his upper arm and heaved a ragged little sigh.

Patrick felt her lean into him and tried not to notice how far he was falling.

"Where do you think the Mercedes is?" Gina asked, comfortably lazy, the thought of their pursuers like some fuzzy notion in the back of her mind.

"Ahead, somewhere," he replied evenly. "I think that by now they realize they got ahead of us last night and are waiting somewhere for us to catch up."

"What'll we do then?"

"Elude them again until I can find the right place to take them on."

"You make it sound easy."

"It's a military trick," he said, rubbing her knee. "Reduce a complicated issue or mission to its simple components and you find that anything can be dealt with if you don't get caught up in the complications."

She leaned her temple against his shoulder. "That sounds like one of those things that isn't as easy in action as it is in theory."

"It all depends on your attitude."

Right now her attitude was too mushy to consider military strategy. She simply leaned against him and watched little clapboard houses go by, boxed-in water towers, split-rail fences from another time, steepled white churches and ruffled, scalloped coves.

"It looks like New England, doesn't it?" she asked. "Maybe we could have our summer home here. What do you think?"

"I think summer's our busiest time in the hotel business," he replied, "and we're not going anywhere. February's a good time to travel, but you'd probably want to go somewhere tropical. I don't think this is a hospitable landscape at that time of year."

She sighed. "Hawaii's so pedestrian. Tahiti's so far."

"What about Mexico?"

She sat up, interested. "I've only been to Mexico City, but I loved it."

"Good," he said, smiling at her enthusiasm. "That settles it. But we should vacation somewhere you haven't been. Acapulco or Cancun."

A strange thought occurred to her and she leaned back against him. "By then we'll only have a month left."

"A month of what?"

"Our marriage. I turn twenty-six in March."

He drove silently for several seconds, then he said philosophically, "Well, you know what they say about the best-laid plans."

She did of course. But was he blithely saying there was little point in planning? Or did the words suggest that the plan on which they'd embarked could easily change and follow another direction entirely?

BY THE TIME he pulled into Rockport, about two-thirds of the way up the California coast, Patrick was beginning to feel as though he'd been born behind the wheel. The two-and-a-half-day drive down to Los Angeles on Interstate 5 had been quick but dull. The last two and a half days had been tediously slow and hair-raising.

He was beginning to feel as though he were dead from the waist down—a sad state of affairs for a groom of three days.

He couldn't wait to find a comfortable motel, eat something that wasn't between two pieces of bread, take a long walk, then take Gina to bed and share with her all the things there hadn't been time for in the hayloft. He smiled as he thought he would also like to repeat a few things there *had* been time for.

"What're you grinning about?" Gina asked. And as she watched, waiting for an answer, his grin froze then died. He made a last-minute turn onto a side street that earned him an emphatic honk and a rude gesture from the driver behind him.

"The Mercedes?" Gina asked, sitting up in her seat, suddenly alert, every vestige of the day's lazy coziness disintegrating.

"I didn't see it," he replied, turning up the street that ran parallel to the main road through town. "But I saw Larry standing on a street corner, smoking a cigar."

"Did he see us?"

"Yeah."

"What now?"

"We do a trade-in."

"A what?"

"Just be ready to move in a hurry."

As they passed the town's main intersection from a parallel street a block away, Gina shouted and pointed, "There they are!"

The black Mercedes was parked in front of a gas station, and Shrimp and Larry were running toward it.

Patrick slowed at the next intersection, then proceeded, racing to the next one, where he made a small sound of satisfaction. "There it is. I saw it from the highway."

"A used-car lot?" Gina asked in surprise, seeing the rows and rows of vehicles that took up most of the block. Then she remembered his remark about a trade-in and frowned at him. "Patrick, the paperwork alone could take..."

"Trust me," he said, and pulled into the truck-and-van section at the back of the lot. A salesman at the other end could be seen pointing out the advantages of a late-model Cadillac to a pair of hot prospects. Patrick and Gina went unnoticed.

"If he's working alone," Patrick said, pulling into a vacant spot between a Ford long-bed and a Cherokee, "we've got it made. Get out and look for something with the keys in it."

"Patrick!" Gina gasped, "Then we'll have the police after us as well as the Mercedes."

He shrugged as though that was a negligible detail. "We're not having much luck getting their help the honest way. Go!"

Patrick took one side of the lot and Gina the other. He kept an eye on the salesman and was relieved by his continued attention on the shopping couple. He blessed the tight economy that probably had him working alone.

But the vehicles on his side of the lot were locked up tight. He was about to race across to help Gina when he spotted the Mercedes doing a slow cruise down the street. He ducked behind a camper shell, trying to spot Gina and warn her. She was nowhere in sight. Now concerned, he crouched toward the back of the camper just in time to have the life scared out of him by a shrill set of brakes and the flat-faced front of an early-seventies Volkswagen bus stopping inches from his nose.

After a breath restored his composure, he saw Gina behind the wheel, grinning broadly and gesturing him to get in.

She was wearing a baseball cap for a feed company that advertised Udder Satisfaction. As the Mercedes rounded the corner out of sight, he climbed into the bus.

"Gina..." he began.

But she wasn't listening. She backed up to the truck with a screech of tires and said urgently. "Get my lamp from the truck."

"Gina..."

"Please!"

The screech had drawn the salesman's attention and there was no time to argue. Cursing the Fates that had gotten him into this, Patrick leapt down from the bus, ran to the truck, fumbled the canopy open, grabbed Gina's precious carton and the blanket and ran back to the bus. She raced forward, blithely ignoring the salesman who stood in the middle of the lot waving both arms.

"Gina..." Patrick warned.

"So what's a little hit-and-run after auto theft and an unpaid motel bill?" she asked calmly as the distance closed between the bus and the salesman.

Patrick was about to reach out for the wheel when she made a sudden turn to the left and exited the lot from a driveway he hadn't noticed. She glanced at him as she made an abrupt turn that slid him toward her. "Just kidding," she said.

"Gina, for God's...!" He began to scold her heatedly when she put a hand to the back of his head and pushed him so that he was doubled over in his seat—and possibly herniated in several places.

"The Mercedes!" she whispered harshly as she pulled up to the stop sign. "Right across from us. Stay down. They're not looking for a woman alone."

"Particularly not one with a hat promising Udder Satisfaction."

"You're just jealous 'cause you don't have a disguise."

"Quit playing around. What's happening?"

"They're staring at me."

"Oh, God."

"Relax. I've always had that effect on men." Gina proceeded toward the main intersection and the Mercedes raced past her, both men looking frantically around, obviously wondering what had become of their prey.

"You can get up now," she said smugly to Patrick. "They fell for it. We're home free."

"Not exactly." Patrick straightened and turned to her with a frown that was both judicious and resigned.

"Why not?" She glanced at him, the brim of the cap darkening her eyes. He swept it off her head.

"Because," he said frustratedly, "now that you've attracted the salesman's attention, he's definitely going to remember us when Larry and Shrimp spot my truck there and go in pretending to be policemen and wanting to know what happened to the felonious driver and his moll."

"Oh." Gina settled back, her shoulders sagging as she followed the highway out of town, picking up speed outside the city limit.

"And," Patrick went on, "we're traveling in a twenty-year-old red Volkswagen that sounds like it's in the last stages of emphysema. It'll be so easy to hide in."

She cast him a dark glance. "You said to look for something with keys in it. All the big-bore V8s with dual carbs were locked up tight. Don't be an ingrate. Uh-oh." The last was delivered in a tone of concern as the bus began to shimmy. She held tight to the wheel to keep it in a straight line. "What's the matter with it?"

"Feels like a bad case of the DTs."

"Patrick!"

Patrick unbuckled his belt. "I think the wheels are out of alignment. Speed up and see if it smooths out."

It didn't. It got worse. She gritted her teeth as the bus shook as though a giant hand were throttling it.

"Try slowing down!" he ordered over the loud racket of rattling seats, dashboard and inside furnishings.

She did, but nothing happened. Patrick slid into the driver's seat behind her and eased her aside, controlling the bucking vehicle while decreasing his foot's pressure on the pedal. At fifty the bus eased back into a comfortable ride. Patrick looked reluctantly into the rearview mirror.

The road behind him was clear. He stared in confused surprise. The black Mercedes should have caught up easily.

"Where the hell are they?" he asked.

When Gina didn't offer a smart reply, he glanced at her to see her staring glumly at him.

The focus of his concern changed abruptly. "What?"

"That means we can't go over fifty," she said worriedly, guiltily.

"It means..." He considered a philosophical way of putting it. "We'll have to be more cunning if we're moving more slowly. That's all."

She raised an eyebrow. "That's all?"

"Trust me. We can do this."

She was hungry and tired, but she didn't want to mention it—this was all her fault, anyway. And the fact that they were now traveling in something that couldn't even do the speed limit was also because of her.

The exhilaration of escape had been quickly eclipsed by the cranky behavior of the bus.

She looked moodily into the glove compartment, found an owner's manual, a flare and a mileage log. She closed it.

"No potato chips?" Patrick teased.

She sighed. "Just dull car stuff."

"Getting hungry?"

"No, I'm fine."

"Liar. You're always hungry." Disturbed by her suddenly quiet mood, he poked a finger at her ribs and was rewarded with an instant giggle. She slapped his hand away and leaned far back in her corner with a look of indignant but amused surprise.

"What are you doing?" she demanded.

"Ticklish, huh?" he said with a speculative grin. "That's something I'll have to take advantage of later."

"What are you so cheerful about?" she asked. "You've been driving for twelve hours on a hamburger and half a bag of potato chips, and we're about to be overtaken by two thugs."

"We're about a hundred and fifty miles from the Oregon border," he said, reaching out companionably to pinch her cheek. "My turf. Then the whole complexion of this will change. Relax. We're almost home."

Home, she thought. Home in his arms—at least for a while. Her mood began to lighten.

As the road turned slightly inland to skirt the King Mountain Range, they passed through a series of small towns just beginning to settle down for the night. The heavy canopy of redwoods brought an early dusk, and as the bus chugged along, lights went on, lining the highway and winking from the shelter of the woods.

"A restaurant!" Gina exclaimed, pointing off the road into a cozy little well of a meadow. "And cabins!" A dozen rustic little cottages were backed up against the trees. Beside them, a little restaurant named Mountain Mama's boasted the best stew around and homemade pie.

Gina's spirits soared. Patrick smiled at the obvious lightening of her mood as he made the turn. He passed the restaurant, following a road that probably led to one of the lights winking in the distance. Halfway up, he nosed the van into the trees and parked.

Gina didn't have to ask why. It was part of his plan to be more cunning now that they were moving more slowly.

They had their pick of cabins, and Patrick chose the corner one nestled into the trees. The stew was hearty and delicious and accompanied by thick corn bread and the best coffee Patrick had had since he'd left home. The pie was apple and as aromatic as a grandmother's kitchen. And the restaurant was open for breakfast at six.

"I've died and gone to heaven," Gina said lazily as she and Patrick walked arm in arm to the cabin, satiated and relaxed. "Now, if we just had a hayloft to sleep in... Patrick!"

She exclaimed in surprise as he unlocked the cabin door, then swept her up in his arms.

"I haven't carried you over the threshold yet," he said, turning sideways to ease her into the room.

"Shall I get the light?" she asked.

"No," he said softly, kicking the door closed behind him. But instead of taking her to the bed as she expected, he took her to the tiny bathroom and set her down in front of the shower. Then he walked back to the door and threw the bolt, securing them from interference from the outside world.

Despite its rustic appearance, the cabin was warm and the shower stall modern, though very small. Patrick started the water, adjusted the temperature, then peeled Gina's clothes from her and put her inside. Dropping his in a pile beside hers, he joined her, closing the stall door and enclosing them in a steamy cocoon. He washed her hair and she washed his, she scrubbed his back and he scrubbed hers, she moved around to the front of him, soaping his pecs, down the center of his chest, along the jut of his ribs—and then he crushed her to him, the soap went flying and her feet were suddenly clear of the shower floor.

As she wrapped her arms tightly around his neck, he braced her thighs around his hips and gently probed inside her with a deftness that made her gasp.

Patrick backed out from under the spray, never ceasing his taunting exploration. In a moment she was quivering like the lights that sparkled in the trees, like the stars in the sky, like the early-morning mountain air.

She opened her mouth over his, hungry for him. That delicious release only made her greedy for more of him, desperate to share what she felt, wild with the need to try to return the pleasure he'd given her—and everything else that had so changed her life in the small space of the last sixty hours.

She felt bound to him, part of him, more connected to his life than she'd ever felt to her own in the past twenty-five years.

He entered her without moving either of them, and she felt herself enfold and embrace him—and felt the same transformation she'd known last night in a hayloft.

Patrick couldn't believe the waves and waves of pleasure that wound through him as the water beat at her back, beat her against him as she swayed and squirmed to be closer, to hold him tighter and take him higher.

Her little cries of distress made him crush her closer and smile to himself. She was fearless and clever and unashamedly hedonistic—and putty in his hands.

A sudden blast of cold water earned a yelp from both of them. Patrick quickly elbowed the door open and set her outside, then fearlessly stepped into the water to turn the taps off.

He stepped out of the shower to be enfolded by Gina in a thick towel. Wrapped in her own, sarong-style, she rubbed warmth into his arms and shoulders and back.

When she came around in front of him, she remembered too late what had happened the last time— or remembered just in time, she thought with a smile as he swept her up and strode with her to the bed.

Chapter Eight

"I'm really tired of this sweater." Gina pulled on the bulky white V-neck she'd worn the past two days and stared disconsolately into the pocked mirror over the cabin's rickety luggage stand. Her image looked back droopily. She put a hand under her hair and held it atop her head, hoping to lift her appearance.

Patrick, walking out of the bathroom, seized the opportunity to kiss the back of her neck. The kiss became a nibble that worked to her shoulder then back up to her ear before he turned her in his arms and kissed her in earnest. "I think you look wonderful," he said.

She leaned back against his laced hands. "You're a liar, but thanks."

He freed one hand to run it over his chin, now dark with two days' growth of beard. "I'm the one looking shaggy."

"Oh, no," she said, running a hand over the wiry stubble, remembering how it had made her body tingle in its most sensitive places. She grinned affectionately. "I like it."

He chuckled. "Ready for breakfast?"

"I'm ready for new clothes," she said disconsolately. "I hate to sound like a whining wife already, but if I don't have something different to put on, and something with which to curl my hair..." She held out a strand of glossy-clean but straight chestnut-colored hair. "I'm going to be very difficult to live with. Worse than I am now."

His eyes widened dramatically. "I'm not sure I could take that. We'll be in Eureka by mid-morning. If there are no surprises on the road, we'll have a brief shopping spree."

She hugged him close. "You're wonderful. Now let me show you my appreciation."

THE MORNING was sunny and cool as Patrick pointed the bus northward. The radio didn't work, but he'd cranked the heat up, refusing Gina's offer to let him wear the jacket for a while. For an hour they were alone on the road.

"It's making me nervous that we haven't spotted them," Gina observed as they drove through miles and miles of sun-dappled woods. "Where do you think they are?"

"Regrouping," he said. "Maybe getting reinforcements. They probably didn't expect you to be as much trouble as you've become." He cast her a grin. "But then, they don't know you like I do."

She huffed, then laughed. "Very funny. Maybe they've just finally decided whatever they were after is too much trouble and they've given up. I still can't imagine what it could be. Who did you call after breakfast this morning?"

"Sin. He has a friend at the Department of Motor Vehicles who's going to try to get us the registry on the Mercedes. Maybe what Shrimp and Larry are after is something you sold off when you cleared out the warehouse. What was there again? That weird lamp, bolts of fabric, a broken chair and . . . what else?"

"A plant stand and a vase. But none of them was anything valuable. And if he'd wanted them, he'd have taken them with him, wouldn't he?"

"Unless he was afraid he might get caught with it. Didn't you say you were putting the pieces together by then and brought the police to the warehouse?"

She thought that through. "Yeah. You mean he was planning to come back for it later?"

Patrick nodded. "And when he did and it was gone, he knew you would know where it was."

"Why didn't he just call me and *speak* to me and get it over with? Why annoy me with phone calls and follow me around?"

"He must think you *know* you have it, whatever it is. The calls were probably just to unsettle you. He followed you, thinking he'd find you trying to sell or hock whatever it is and he could handle it from there himself when you'd gone. He *kept* following you because you didn't do anything with it, and he kept waiting for you to.''

Gina leaned back and closed her eyes, thinking through the items she'd found in a heap in the middle of the warehouse floor, discarded, she'd thought, as too inexpensive to claim Yale's attention.

Unless there'd been something about one of them she simply hadn't seen or been aware of.

''You're sure there's nothing valuable about your lamp?'' Patrick asked.

She didn't have to consider. ''Positive. It's nothing but plaster and glass beads. I love it for its significance to me alone, not its value.''

He snaked an arm across her lap and tucked his hand under her knee. ''The middle of the rainbow, huh?''

She leaned into him. ''Right.'' And I think I've found it, she thought in wonder.

They passed a road sign that read Eureka—eighteen miles.

''Almost shopping-spree time,'' Patrick said. ''Do me a favor?''

''What?''

''Buy more of that smoky gray underwear.''

She laughed softly against his upper arm. ''You took it off me so fast I thought you didn't like it.''

''It matches your eyes,'' he said, glancing away from the road for an instant, his eyes alight with a vivid memory, ''and when it's all you're wearing, it's like being lost in a cloudy heaven.''

She dissolved against him. "I'll buy everything gray, how's that?"

"Unwise," he replied. "When we get home, I'll be expected to function in my usually efficient and competent manner. I won't be able to unless the gray you're wearing is covered up and waiting for me to discover it in the privacy of our home."

She sighed as the scenery rolled by. "You're making it hard for me to remember there's a time limit on this relationship."

"I've always ignored limits," he said lightly. "Or constraints of any kind."

She raised her head to look at his profile in surprise. "Surely the Marine Corps didn't let you do that?"

"Every man accepts a certain authority over his life," he said, guiding the bus easily as the road rose and curved. "But within those parameters, you set your own rules. And anyway, the corps doesn't own me anymore. No one does."

A subtle reminder, she wondered. She didn't want to think about it. At that moment she wanted nothing in the world but to sit beside him in a loud and slow but cozy VW bus winding through a beautiful mountain road on the way to a shopping trip. Except for the black Mercedes, she thought, life was about as close to perfect as it could get.

EUREKA WAS a lively little town with absolutely everything they needed. When Gina fingered the contents of a new rack of summery shirts and pants, Patrick pushed her to what remained of the winter wear. "Turtlenecks, jeans, sweats, woolly socks," he said. "Candle Bay isn't sunny Southern California. You'll need warm clothes until late June, early July."

She found a blow dryer and curling iron and new makeup.

"I kind of like you without that stuff," Patrick said when he met her at the cosmetics counter and she asked for his credit card.

The clerk gave Gina a jealous look as she handed the card over.

There was some discussion over who should buy the new jacket.

Patrick pointed to the leather one he'd lent her. "It's way too big," he said. "You have to push the sleeves up and you could wrap it around you twice."

They stood in the men's department, and she turned to the three-way mirror. With her hair caught up in a new banana clip, and with no makeup, she looked about thirteen but, she thought, very chic.

"I like it. It's very fashionable. The big look is in and sleeves are always pushed up." She turned away from the mirror and perused the racks. She finally stopped at a rack of tweed stadium jackets, pulled down a black-and-gray one and held it for Patrick to slip into.

After they paid, they went to have coffee and bought a bag of donuts and muffins to take with them. "Just in case," Patrick said as they climbed into the bus. "You peering into an empty glove compartment is not a pretty sight."

Gina laughed and thought she might die of happiness.

"Oh, my new curling iron!" she exclaimed, looking over her packages again to make sure she hadn't put it in a bigger bag. Then she remembered. "I set everything down in the bakery to look at the display case."

In the act of snapping his seat belt in place, Patrick stopped and slipped out of it. "I remember," he said with a wry glance her way as he leapt out of the bus. "It was embarrassing when you pushed those little children out of the way. Wait here. I'll be right back."

"I didn't push them out of the way. I just asked them to move so I could get a better look at the Danish."

"Yeah, right. The little boy ended up sprawled on the day-old bread rack and the little girl's probably still flying."

She grinned and rolled her eyes at his exaggeration. "Will you go get my stuff before someone else picks it up?"

He turned back to add, "If you spot our 'friends,' honk the horn."

"Right."

Patrick was becoming concerned because he was having a good time. He shouldn't be. He should be taut and vigilant and aware of the possibility of danger at every turn.

Instead his mind was filled with Gina and the sensory memory of the last two nights in her arms. He'd been anticipating nightfall since he'd awakened that morning.

He knew he had it bad because all her little quirks didn't annoy him.

Love, he wondered? A scary proposition, but he always faced the truth. He'd spent a lifetime being stronger and tougher than everything else that came his way.

He shouldered his way into the bakery and decided to think about that later. The clerk behind the counter remembered him instantly and pointed to the corner near an umbrella stand where the package still stood. He scooped it up with a wave of thanks and pushed his way out the door.

Fear lodged in his throat the moment he stepped onto the sidewalk. Parked two spots up the street was an empty black Mercedes. It hadn't been there when he'd walked into the bakery. And Gina hadn't hit the horn.

As he pressed back into the bakery doorway, his eyes flew to the bus, parked halfway down the street. He felt a sharp clutch of fear as he saw that it, too, was empty.

He started to sidle toward it through the spare midmorning foot traffic when he saw Shrimp and Larry approach the bus from the street side. He ducked into the front of a sporting-goods shop and watched as

Larry tried the door and Shrimp walked the length of the bus, peering in through the windows.

At any moment he expected a shout of victory from the big man when he spotted Gina. But it didn't come. He began to wonder if they'd already taken her, maybe put her in the trunk of the Mercedes.

Panic fought with common sense and he had to assert his experience and training to keep his emotions in check. If they had her, they wouldn't be hanging around. And he doubted they would bother looking for him. Still, he wouldn't be able to draw another breath until he knew.

Gina saw them coming, he told himself, and left the bus to hide. But why hadn't she honked the horn?

Shrimp and Larry looked around, exchanged a few words, then separated, one on each side of the street, apparently to begin a methodical, store-by-store search.

Shrimp took the bakery side of the street. Patrick hid behind an inflated rubber raft while Shrimp started into a drugstore. The big man was driven back by a group of young girls in very short skirts, arms loaded down with packages, hair teased into pointed spikes.

Shrimp gave them a wide berth and headed back into the shop. About to try to make it to the van and begin his own search for Gina, Patrick noticed a certain familiarity to one of the pair of legs.

As he watched, the owner of the legs handed a tall bag to one of the other girls and separated herself from the group. She slipped the sunglasses down her nose and looked anxiously up and down the street. Gina!

God! She'd bumped elbows with Shrimp! He wanted to hug her because she was safe, then he wanted to kill her. Patrick pulled the collar of his jacket up and made his way quickly but calmly toward her. She had started to move toward the bus. Then she spotted him and ran to him.

"Patrick," she said, grabbing his arm, "they're—"

"I know." He turned her swiftly to the bus, snapped, "Get in and get down!" then ran across the street to the Mercedes. He lifted the hood, removed the distributor cap and tossed it aside, then ran back to the bus and leapt into the driver's seat. He knew the moment he turned the key in the ignition he would have Larry's attention. Nothing else in the world could be mistaken for a VW engine.

He turned the key, the engine percolated loudly and he pulled out into the street. Through the rearview mirror he saw Larry come running out of a florist shop and race to the middle of the street. His features were growing too distant to be distinguishable, but the fist shaken at their exhaust wasn't. He grinned as he realized how the gesture would change when Larry realized the car wouldn't start.

Patrick did his best to eat up the road—or, in the case of the Volkswagen, at least nibble at it—while he could. It kept him from killing Gina.

GINA, brushing her hair back into order and tissuing makeup off her face, knew something was wrong apart from the fact that the black Mercedes had almost caught them. Patrick looked positively severe as he stared at the road, sparing only an occasional glance in the rearview mirror. And never one in her direction.

Not yet recovered from the fright she felt when she saw the Mercedes approaching through the makeup mirror, she was in no mood to baby *his* mood.

"What?" she demanded when they'd driven fifteen miles without speaking. "Tell me. How did this get to be my fault?"

He still didn't look at her. "We'll talk about it," he said in an ominously quiet voice, "when I can forget the image of you bumping elbows with Shrimp. You just have to push everything to the edge, don't you? You had to bump into him to show yourself just how close you could get with your clever little disguise."

"Oh, it's the disguise thing again, is it?" she asked angrily, forgetting to explain how the scenario had come about. "Well, next time we'll be sure and get *you* one. You get so testy when I have one and you don't."

"Gina..." There was warning in his tone, but she was too upset to hear it.

"We'll get you one," she went on, "the next time that I have three minutes to save my hide and you're nowhere to be found!"

"I went for the package *you* carelessly left in the bakery," he retorted, his voice beginning to rise. "Remember?"

"Well, pardon me! You're the one who made the decision to leave all our stuff in a Santa Cruz motel room. If I hadn't had to carry all the things we bought, maybe I wouldn't have forgotten some of it."

He shouted an oath. "I asked you to hold them while I paid for the half-dozen donuts that would keep *you* quiet until lunch!"

"So I have a healthy appetite!" she shouted back. "Five hundred thousand dollars will pay for a *lot* of donuts! Maybe I could expect a little tolerance."

"Why? It's your father's money. You blew yours through mistaken friendship and bad judgment!"

"Well, apparently that wasn't the only time I've exercised bad judgment!"

There was a moment's pulsing silence. "Hey," he said easily, "you've got a clear way out anytime you want it."

"Fine!" She was cut to the quick. Only moments ago she'd been thinking about how happy she was and how, for the first time in her life, her future looked promising. It had taken a very short time to change all that. "Fine. Just stop and let me out. Anywhere along here will be fine."

Patrick ignored her and continued to drive, always checking the rearview mirror for any sign of the Mercedes. He would settle with her the moment he felt sure they were in the clear.

"Maybe you're deaf as well as irascible," she said quietly. "I asked you to let me out."

He shook his head at the absurdity of her request. "You may take my silence as refusal to comply."

"Fine." She put a hand out to reach for her door handle. He had her other one in a steel grip so fast he stopped her action.

"Put that hand down," he ordered, "or you'll wish I'd let you out, so help me."

Her hand remained suspended, but she glared at him despite the pain in the hand he held. "So you turn out to have a brutal side," she said.

He glanced at the road then back at her. "You want to see it?" he asked tightly.

She was more than happy to push him. She tugged on the handle and the door opened.

She'd never intended to leap from the bus. She'd been sure he would pull over the moment she opened her door. But the wind caught it and the door swung wide, pulling her with it. Pavement flew by at a startling speed.

She heard Patrick's shout, but for an instant she could do nothing but watch in fascination as the fog line streaked past. Then a yank she was sure had dislocated her shoulder pulled her back into the bus.

Patrick lost the fragile hold he'd kept on his control. Still holding Gina's arm, he pulled off the road and cut the motor.

He turned to her, fury in his eyes and in his grip. "You insufferable brat!" he shouted. "You don't need a contemporary husband, you need a nineteenth-century man who would take you over his knee and show you what your attention-getting games will earn you."

She knew she was courting danger, but that seemed to be what life with him was all about. And he hadn't once bothered to ask her what had happened—he had simply accused.

She raised a haughty eyebrow. "I guess the classic line here is, 'You wouldn't dare!' But you might remember where the money comes from in this relationship before you make up your mind."

She should have remembered he was a decisive man. One moment they were face-to-face, and the next he sat where she'd been and she was suspended over his knee, her legs trapped under the dash.

"Patrick!" she cried in mortified surprise.

"If you'll remember..." His voice drifted down to her as she stared at the bus's old blue carpet and her clutch purse lying on its side. She struggled but a hard hand on her hipbone held her in place. "You don't have a dime until next March, and my check's already cashed and being distributed. I would dare, Gina."

He tightened his grip on her. She gasped and tensed, waiting for the first blow to fall.

Patrick heard the little sound, felt her fist clench on the thigh of his jeans and decided he'd made his point. He yanked her up and sat her down firmly in the driver's seat.

Her cheeks were flushed, her eyes overbright with anger and embarrassment. But he had her full attention.

"I *would* dare," he said again. "In fact, for your own safety, the next time, I probably should. But I apparently have more respect for you than you have for me."

Tears pooled in her eyes, but she willed them not to fall.

"I'd never deliberately hurt you," he went on, his voice calmer, "but *you* scared the hell out of me twice in the space of twenty minutes."

A tear fell, anyway. Furious at him, mad at herself, she swiped it away and folded her arms. "The horn didn't work," she said quickly because her voice was unsteady.

"What?" He frowned, forgetting for a moment what the horn had to do with it.

"You said if I saw them, to honk the horn." She remembered sharply how frightened she'd been for him. "I tried. It didn't work." She angled him a judicious glare and looked away from him.

He reached out to slap the palm of his hand against the horn. It didn't work. It was one of the vehicle's features he hadn't tried since they'd "liberated" it.

He fought feelings of guilt by remembering her pushing the bus door open and nearly falling out.

"Don't look so righteous," he scolded. "You opened the door of a moving vehicle."

She turned to him, fire under the tears in her eyes. "You *accused* me of playing games! When I couldn't warn you by honking the horn, I was going to come for you, only they got out of the car before I could reach the bakery. So I ducked into the drugstore."

He frowned, trying to unravel her meaning. "Why didn't you just stay where you were safe?"

She looked at him as though he was dim. "Because I was worried about *you* bumping into them."

"I told you to honk the horn," he said, "so I could come to protect *you*. You were not expected to come and protect *me*."

"Well, if it's any comfort," she said, looking away from him again, "I'm sorry I did. I should have let you get shot or hauled away or whatever they have in mind."

She really had left the bus to save him. His anger was beginning to dissipate. But it wasn't gone.

"What," he asked, "does that have to do with opening the door of a moving vehicle?"

She sighed heavily and shook her head. "I was angry. I'm not always rational when I'm mad."

He reached across the space that separated them and pulled her into his lap. "All right. We've made each other angry and learned it isn't wise. We still have a ways to go. We have to do it in harmony, or we're not going to make it. Agreed?"

She gave him a warning gray glance. "If you're going to ask me to kiss you, forget it."

"I wasn't going to ask," he said, then took a kiss that gave her everything she needed at that moment. It was filled with passion, strength and tenderness.

It was easy to kiss him back, to wrap her arms around him and lose herself in his embrace.

She felt herself relax as his strong hand rubbed gently up and down her spine.

"I'm sorry I made the crack about the money," she said, planting a kiss under his ear.

He rubbed a hand gently along her bare thigh. "It's all right. I'm sorry I made the crack about the donuts. Incidentally..." He fingered the little scrap of delicate black fabric that barely covered the tops of her thighs. "Where'd you get the skirt? You were wearing sweats when I left you and all the stuff we bought was in the bus."

"It's not a skirt," she said, tugging on it to show him it was attached to the brief panties under it. "It's the skirt of my teddy. I bought it today, too, but I liked it so much I left it on."

"Where are the sweats?"

"I had them tucked in my jacket. I tossed them in the back while you were busy messing under the hood of the Mercedes."

He sighed and rubbed a hand gently along the silky skin from knee to torso. "Well, you'd better put them on again if we're ever going to make the Oregon border."

She slipped off his lap and he resumed his place behind the wheel. When she bent to reach her sweats, he took advantage of the opportunity to swat her backside.

She turned to him with a frown.

"Just a reminder," he said as he turned the key and the motor coughed to life, "never to reach for the door handle in a moving vehicle."

Chapter Nine

Gina felt as though she'd passed into a parallel universe when they crossed the Oregon border. She wondered if it was the suggestion that they'd almost reached Patrick's "turf" and some kind of safety that made the trees greener, the sky bluer, even the fat pewter clouds seem friendly.

"I'm glad you talked me into turtlenecks instead of halter tops," she said as they parked the van two blocks off the highway in Brookings and walked back to a little restaurant off the water.

A cold wind whipped around them, salty and fragrant. Gina tried to walk around the restaurant for a clearer view of the driftwood strewn on the beach, but Patrick pulled her back.

"No time for that," he said. "My guess is that when the Mercedes didn't start, they found another car. The next time they close in on us, we won't have the advantage of knowing they're coming." He'd decided to have the oak doors shipped, after all. The weight would slow the bus down considerably.

Gina placed their order while Patrick made a phone call. He came back to the table with a frown.

"The Mercedes is registered to R. P. Danforth," he said. "That name mean anything to you?"

She repeated it to herself, waiting for memory to kick in. It didn't. "No." She sipped at her coffee and shook her head. "That's weird. Why would someone I don't even know be after me for something I don't have?"

"Or don't know you have."

"I know," she insisted, "I don't have it. Apparently whatever they wanted wasn't in all the luggage we left behind in Santa Cruz. If it's someone Yale is connected with, the lamp and all the other stuff in the warehouse was obviously worthless to him because he left it. What else is there? Just . . . me."

Patrick's dark eyes locked on her, moody, faintly self-deprecating and curiously resigned. "Well, now you're mine. I'll just have to make that clearer to him once we cross paths again."

She patted his hand teasingly. "You should have fallen for some leggy Oregon girl who knows all about fishing and doesn't have people chasing her all over the country."

He shook his head. "Sounds dull. After the military, I have a thirst for adventure. Eat your lunch. We can make it to Newport tonight."

GINA STRAINED at her seat belt for a better view of the wild coast as they headed for Newport. Towering mountains pitched steeply into the ocean; surf battered against craggy bluffs spewing foam in dramatic displays. Long stretches of smooth sand and beautiful little harbors went on and on.

Then there were miles of sand dunes. "Look at the dune buggies!" Gina pointed to the spots of color crawling up and down the shifting landscape like bugs in a garden.

Patrick glanced away from the road, studied the dune buggies with disapproval and nodded. "If I were king," he said with a facetious smile, "I wouldn't allow anything with a motor on the sand."

"Erosion?"

He nodded again. "And mental erosion. Water washing on the sand, sand drifting, sea gulls calling, sandpipers running, are for enjoying without the interference of blaring noise. The beach should be for thinking and dreaming and restoring yourself."

She studied his grave profile in pleased surprise. "That's a poetic thought for a former soldier turned businessman."

He shrugged a shoulder. "Life and death make you philosophical. I suppose you grew up on water skis on the back of a motorboat."

She shook her head. "No. I grew up on a tennis court. Do you play?"

He nodded. "We have two on the hotel grounds. We'll have to settle all our arguments there."

"How do you know we'll have any?"

He smiled at the road. "We've had three already and we've only been married three days."

"This is our fourth day," she corrected.

"I apologize. Four days. That's not a hopeful average, do you think?"

She turned toward him and leaned her elbow on the back of her seat. "When you're being chased by hoodlums, it's probably not a bad average. I'm generally in a good mood. And you seem to be," she added, teasing carefully, "as long as no one does anything to frighten you."

He took the gentle criticism with a smile that had an edge of warning in it. "Remember that. You given any thought to what you'll need to help me with the child-care facility?"

She delved into the little clutch that went everywhere with her. "I've made some notes."

"You have?" he asked in surprise. "When?"

"Various times. Before we got married. Day before yesterday while you made the phone call to Sin. Yesterday morning, before you got up."

That surprised him into silence for a moment.

"So what did you conclude while I was asleep?" he asked.

She consulted a small leather-bound book. "We'll need the obvious. Bright paint, indoor-outdoor carpet, a carpenter who won't mind doing some 'fun' stuff."

"Fun stuff?"

"Small furniture, cubbyholes, hidey-holes, lockers for the children's things."

"Ah."

"Books," she went on. "Toys, craft stuff, pillows and blankets, and if the budget'll stretch that far, a VCR and movies."

He nodded slowly, marveling that she'd obviously given the project enough thought to have a pretty thorough idea of what she planned to do. Any notion he might have had that she'd do a halfhearted job was put to rest.

"Sounds good," he said. "We'll go over it when we get there. I've got two rooms that might serve. You can decide which one."

Gina tucked her notebook back into her purse and put it aside. "And when I'd finished making my notes," she said softly, "I watched you sleep."

That statement hung in the air in the confinement of the bus, gently suggestive, further unsettling. "Really," he said.

"Yes." She propped her head on her hand and studied him. She liked the little lines on his forehead. "You were frowning..." She reached a hand out and touched his forehead just above the bridge of his nose. "Just like you are now."

"Must have been wondering what to do with you," he said, sparing her a quick, unreadable glance. "Just like I am now."

"Mmm. Did you dream a solution?"

"You wouldn't want to hear about it," he said with a straight face. "It involved a gag and handcuffs."

PULLING INTO a rest stop a little while later, Patrick perused the map on the kiosk that listed tourist attractions on the coast, while Gina went to the rest room. Then he walked back to lean against the wall in front of the ladies' room and wait.

He frowned, thinking that for a woman who usually didn't dawdle in the bathroom, Gina was taking an awfully long time. He straightened, suddenly concerned.

"Gina?" he called.

She answered instantly. "Yeah?"

Relief relaxed him. "You 'bout ready?"

"A few more minutes," she shouted back. "I'm curling my hair."

"What?" He couldn't believe what he'd heard.

"I'm curling my hair," she repeated. "This Oregon dampness is making my ends frizzy."

He closed his eyes and counted to five. He didn't have time to make it to ten. "Gina!" he barked. "You're being chased by hoods and you're curling your hair? I'm going to frizz your other end if you don't move it!"

"Honestly," she said after a moment, her tone slightly injured. "I refuse to look a frump, even when I'm running for my life. I thought you were an understanding husband. I'll just be another minute."

He paused to count again, and that was when he
heard the low purr of a powerful motor. It was cruis-
ing, not racing, and it was coming from the picnic
shelter where he'd concealed the bus.

He hid himself behind the ladies'-room wall and
watched as a buglike red Corvette cruised up the road
from the camper side of the rest stop. A man of small
stature drove, and the passenger's seat was empty.
Patrick wasn't fooled. He'd used the trick of hiding his
passenger enough times himself in the past few days.

He ran into the ladies' room, past Gina who still
stood in front of the mirror, and into the stall directly
below the air vent.

"Gina! Get over here!" he ordered as he clam-
bered onto the seat, braced a foot on the paper dispenser and propelled himself onto the wall that
separated the cubicles. Supporting himself with a grip
on a light fixture, he slapped the flat of his hand
against the vent. It didn't give. He heard the hum of
the Corvette grow louder.

He hit it again and again and it finally flew upward
with a loud clatter. The hum was now right outside the
rest-room door.

Gina scrambled up after him, stood on the toilet
seat, reached up to grab the top of the wall and hoist
herself to plant a foot on the paper dispenser as he'd
done.

One hand braced in the open hole, Patrick reached
the other down to her and hauled her up beside him to
stand on the narrow ledge of the wall. She wobbled

precariously and he held her steady until she was balanced. Then he pulled himself up through the hole.

With pounding heart, Gina heard the slam of car doors, the sound of voices. Patrick reached down for her and she clutched his biceps for dear life. For an instant, she was just plain tired of the struggle. Then the awkward position reminded her of being hauled up into the hayloft. It gave her a suddenly different perspective on her situation. She walked her feet up the wall as he pulled and suddenly found herself on the slanted cedar roof of the rest room. Soundlessly Patrick replaced the air vent.

Knees braced against the pitch of the roof, Gina and Patrick lay back, listening to the conversation as Larry and Shrimp checked out the men's room, then the ladies'.

"Well, where the hell are they?" Larry's sharp voice.

"Maybe they stole another car," Shrimp said.

"Stupid. They'd have taken their stuff with them. It's still in the bus."

"They left their stuff before."

"No, they're here. I know it. I'm sure. All we gotta do is find 'em."

"Why don't we call the bo—"

"I'm not calling the boss again until I have her neck in my hand. Remember what he said last time."

There was an audible swallow. "We find 'em, or... nobody'll ever find us."

"Right. Start looking. Check everything everywhere. Start with the woods behind the rest room. I'm going across to the beach."

"Okay, Larry."

Clearly visible against the roof of the rest room, Patrick and Gina watched Shrimp lumber off into the thick trees, a gun clearly visible in his hand. He never once looked back over his shoulder. Gina breathed a sigh of relief when he disappeared.

"I hope," she whispered, "you've called for a helicopter to pluck us off the roof."

"Sorry." Patrick inched his way to the edge and looked down. "Piece o' cake," he said, turning to wave her to follow him. "Come on." He disappeared in a nimble leap.

Gina crab-walked to the edge and discovered that Patrick's piece o' cake was a considerable drop to asphalt. He waited, arms raised to receive her.

"Jump!" he whispered harshly, beckoning to her.

"Oh, God!" she grumbled under her breath, rolling onto her stomach and easing her legs and backside over the edge. She gripped with her fingers as she hung the length of her arms.

Patrick's hands clamped on to her calves. "I've got you. Let go!"

According to all reasonable laws of physics, she was sure the upper part of her body would pitch forward, she would tumble out of Patrick's precarious hold and land headfirst in the daffodils that bordered the rest room.

She was surprised to find trust more reliable than physics. She let go and Patrick's arms immediately snaked around her as she fell, one around her hips, the other just under her breasts. He eased her to the asphalt, caught her hand, and they headed off at a run toward the bus.

She heard Shrimp's shout behind them before they were halfway across the clearing toward the shelter of trees and the bus. They kept running.

The bus looked as though it had fallen into a hole. As Patrick jerked her to a stop, Gina stared at the vehicle that appeared to be sitting a foot lower than it had when they'd left it. She noticed the slashed tires just as Patrick whispered a pithy one-word assessment of their situation.

He yanked her around the bus and toward the woods. Breath was already burning in her lungs.

"Is this where I tell you bravely to leave me behind and save yourself?" she asked as she pumped after him for all she was worth.

"No, this is where you shut up," he retorted, slapping an overhanging branch aside as they ran into the shelter of Oregon firs, "and save your breath for running."

They continued to run. She ducked and dodged, fully expecting to get a faceful of bark at any moment.

She heard shouting and footsteps pounding behind them. Patrick took a left down a slimy slope. She followed, losing her footing. He caught her at the waist as she fell and pinned her there with his body, a leg slung over her to prevent her from sliding. He put a finger to his lips for silence. She nodded, but couldn't help gasping for breath.

They were just below the lip of the slope, she noted with a backward glance over her head. Footsteps pounded past.

When they'd gone, she stirred under Patrick, expecting him to leap up and lead the way back to the rest area. He shook his head at her and clamped a hand over her mouth.

Then she realized what was wrong. It had been only one pair of footsteps. Another came along more slowly and with considerably less sound. Larry.

Still pinned under Patrick with his hand over her mouth, Gina looked up at him, praying that he wasn't going to do what he appeared to have in mind. She watched his alert eyes track the sound just above their heads, saw the anger and the time-to-get-even look in them as the footsteps paused before going on.

She shook her head at him frantically, hoping to discourage him from his plan.

Patrick saw the fear for him in Gina's eyes and looked away from it, unwilling to consider it. He'd had it. The showdown was here and now. What had been for a while an interesting little adventure was becoming a pain in the butt. He wanted to get on with his life. He wanted to get on with Gina.

He waited until Larry was several feet past him, then he leapt silently up the slope. He was on him before he knew what happened. With any luck, he'd own Larry's gun before Shrimp even heard the fracas.

He hadn't been out of the military long enough to forget that luck was seldom on your side, but he was reminded sharply, anyway, when he had Larry pinned to the ground and heard Gina's scream.

Distracted, he took a knee to the gut and was suddenly looking down the barrel of a Colt .45.

A moment later Gina struggled up over the rim of the slope, her clothes muddy, dead leaves in her hair.

"I fell down the...slope," she said, hesitating as she looked at the obvious result of her distracting scream. Still breathing hard, she dropped her head onto her arms and groaned.

Larry encouraging him with an upward motion of the barrel of the gun, Patrick got to his feet and pulled her up beside him. This was going to require a few dangerous moves. He wished Gina were still at the bottom of the slope.

"Okay, so where is it?" Larry said testily, obviously as tired of the long northward trek as they were. He put the gun to Patrick's temple. "I want it in my hand now or I'm going to pollute this beautiful wayside with your brains."

Patrick pushed Gina to the side and backed away, hoping to draw Larry with him. "We don't have it," he said.

"Yes, you do," Larry cocked a bullet into the chamber. "The boss says you do."

"We left it on the road."

Larry considered that possibility with a frown, then shook his head, an angry tick beginning in his jaw. "You wouldn't do that. That would be stupid, and if there's anything you ain't, it's *stupid!* Now where is it?"

Patrick would have preferred to be a little farther from Gina. The gun could discharge when he hit him, but Larry was getting too itchy to dawdle with him any longer.

Patrick was just psyching himself to put everything he had into his right fist when Gina ran to him, interposing herself between him and Larry. She flattened her back against his chest and put both arms out protectively.

"Don't you threaten him," she said angrily. "He has nothing to do with this! He doesn't even know where I put it." That sounded believable, she thought frantically. Of course, *she* didn't know where she'd put it, either, because she didn't know what "it" was. She spared Larry that detail.

"Gina!" Patrick took one of her extended arms and spun her away from him with it while Larry looked on in confusion. Patrick pointed a finger at her. "You stay out of it!" he said, trying to convey with a look that he had a plan if she would just let him get to it.

He was not surprised when his silent communication conveyed nothing.

She flew back at him again, this time standing on tiptoe to wrap her arms around his neck and resist his efforts to dislodge her.

"You'll have to shoot me to get to him," she said to Larry, though she was looking at Patrick. "And then how will you find it?"

While Larry wondered about that, Patrick yanked Gina to the left and landed his right fist in Larry's face. The gun went flying and so did Larry. He landed with a thud and didn't move.

"What did you do to Larry?" Shrimp demanded, stepping into the clearing, his shaking gun pointed at Patrick. He walked to his partner's inert frame and nudged it with his toe. "I got lost, Larry. Are you okay?"

"I killed him," Patrick said, wishing he hadn't been worried about Gina and had watched which way Larry's gun had flown. He had one course of action left. When you didn't have a weapon, you had to have presence.

He strode toward Shrimp as though four men armed with M16s followed him. "Just like I'm going to kill you," he said, never taking his eyes off the quaking hand holding the gun. "Unless you give that to me. Now."

Shrimp handed the Smith and Wesson automatic over without a second thought. Patrick turned to

Gina. "Run back to the rest rooms and see if there's a trucker there who can call the state police for us."

"BOTH MEN deny knowledge of Gardner or Danforth," the state trooper said. Patrick and Gina sat in chairs facing his desk in the office at Newport. "They said they just targeted you as a wealthy couple and thought they'd share your traveler's checks."

Patrick closed his eyes and summoned patience. He was just beginning to understand Gina's frustration in getting law enforcement to help her. "We've traveled the last six hundred miles in a twenty-year-old Volkswagen bus. Would that make us sound like good pickings to you? And if they wanted to steal from us, why didn't they break into the van?"

"They slashed the tires," the trooper reminded.

"To disable it so we couldn't get away," Gina said. "We're telling you this isn't about theft. They've followed us from Los Angeles. And they'd been following me long before that. They want me!"

"Why?"

"I don't know. They're after something I'm supposed to have."

"What?"

Gina looked helplessly at Patrick and subsided in her chair. "I don't know," she replied, defeated.

"And you have no witnesses to these previous attempts to kidnap you?"

"The hotel manager in Santa Cruz," Patrick said. "Did you call him?"

The trooper nodded. "He never heard of you. Says you're not on his register."

"We left owing him seventy-two dollars," Gina cried. "He *has* to remember us."

At the trooper's raised eyebrow, Patrick stood and pulled Gina to her feet. "They bought him off. Big surprise."

"Well, I've got both of them on violation of parole because of their weapons. Both have petty theft and assault records. I'm afraid that's the best I can do for you right now." He smiled genially. "Have a pleasant trip."

A pleasant trip. Patrick looked at Gina, saw the utter frustration of the past two hours registered in her eyes, and was surprised to find himself needing to laugh. When he smiled, her mood changed quickly, as though she'd just been looking for an excuse. They left the office arm in arm, laughing hysterically.

"IT DOESN'T FEEL like it's over, does it?" Gina asked wearily. She lay back against Patrick's chest in an old ball-and-claw bathtub in a Victorian bed-and-breakfast outside of Newport. The tub was filled with herby-smelling bubbles, and Gina soaped the arm with which Patrick held her to him.

"No," he said, raising his other arm to hold her so that she could sponge off the soapy one. "Because, technically, it isn't. Though Shrimp and Larry will probably do time, I'm sure whoever is after whatever it is will be back. But I have security people at the hotel, and until this is resolved, you're not going anywhere without me or one of my people."

That should rankle, Gina thought, but the past four days had taught her to respect and value his protection.

She soaped his other arm. "I suppose after what I've put you through you're already thinking about divorce," she said.

The hand that held her to him gently stroked her breast. She felt the little shudder of thrill deep inside. "Do I look as though I've hired a lawyer?" he asked.

She soaped the second arm. "You certainly have grounds. And your contract with my father was verbal, not written."

"I promised." He took the sponge from her and tossed it to the foot of the tub. It landed with a plop and a spray of suds. He brought her back even closer to assure himself of her attention. "I don't have to sign my name to feel committed to the deal—in business or in marriage."

She leaned her head into his shoulder, feeling warm and safe, but suffering a nagging pang of guilt. "I hate to think of you planning a big party in your remodeled hotel while worrying if your wife is going to be snatched from under your nose at any moment, ruining everything and probably getting you a lot of bad press.''

"Nothing gets snatched from me,'' he said, turning her so that she knelt astride him. "If Gardner or Danforth or whoever the hell is behind this shows up, we'll be ready for him and you'll be safe.''

"But what if—?''

"Your job,'' he interrupted, "is to concentrate on getting the day care ready, and try to make the adjustment from California girl to Oregon woman.''

She leaned forward on him, smiling when she saw the ready passion smolder in his eyes. "You think there's really a difference?''

He combed the damp tendrils of her hair back with his fingers, his eyes consuming her face, feature by feature. "There has to be. We raise no hothouse flowers here. Those of us born in Oregon have that strain of stubborn, sturdy pioneer who came thousands of miles in search of something that couldn't be found in the neat, quiet streets east of St. Louis.''

"You run an elegant hotel,'' she reminded him. "Would your sturdy pioneer ancestry approve of that?''

"Of course.'' Unable to stop himself, he kissed her eyelashes. "Those who visit Oregon come for the same

things as those who live here are after—gracious living on the edge of the wilderness. Oregon is settled but
it isn't tame." His lips moved to her mouth and
opened over it. He kissed her deeply and hard, then
withdrew, the smolder in his eyes igniting. "And that's
the way we like our women."

Chapter Ten

"Oh!" Gina breathed, once again feeling as though she were trapped in a fairy tale. Patrick had stopped on a knoll overlooking Candle Bay and the inn his family had operated since the turn of the century.

The inn was a red-roofed masterpiece of Queen Anne architecture with a main, central building two stories high in classic Victorian style.

"Downstairs are the administration offices, the front desk, a dining room, the lounge and bar. Upstairs are rooms." He pointed to two long, low buildings, obviously later additions, that snaked down to the water from either side. A network of scaffolding was mounted against them, and Gina noticed molded fretwork trim being installed to match that of the main building. "Those are also rooms and that round building on the water with the cupola is a ballroom for special parties. A lot of local people use it."

A completely new two-story building was under construction, tucked against the hillside. "More rooms," he said, "and a cappuccino bar."

Beyond the ballroom was a dock and a small marina with three good-size fishing boats.

The whole was laid out against a rare sunny April day, white clouds scudding across a bright blue sky over an even bluer bay.

Gina noticed a fussy little building near the marina, reroofed like all the others.

"Boathouse," Patrick explained. "We don't use it much. Our newer boats with the flying bridges are too tall for it. But it's so charming, I hate to take it down."

As they watched the riverbank, a heron rose and made its strangely graceful, awkward way across the bay.

Its flight led Gina's eyes to the hilly, fir-covered terrain across the water. Commercial buildings and an old power-plant stack rimmed the bank, and colorful houses dotted the hillside. Sunlight glinted off moving traffic and windows of homes nestled in the trees.

"What's that?" she asked, pointing.

"Astoria," he replied. "Oldest settlement west of the Rockies."

"It's beautiful from here."

"You should see it at night. It looks like a pirate's treasure trove, a mound of jewels in the dark." He put an arm around her and squeezed her shoulder. "Come on, I'll show you the house."

Gina couldn't quite believe it. The house, on a terrace between the hotel and the top of the knoll, was built in the same Queen Anne style, one round turret-like gable on one end of the house, surrounded by a screened-in crescent-shaped porch. There were rounded columns where the porch straightened across the front, and big, double oak doors with leaded-glass windows.

"It's in desperate need of repair," Patrick said, unlocking the door. "My grandfather had been alone for the last thirty years of his life and preferred to live at the hotel. So far I've had my hands full keeping things going there and have paid little attention to the house. One of the hotel maids tidies it for me a couple of times a week, but that's all the care it's gotten. The plumbing's iffy, the wiring's reliable but a little spare, and it needs paint desperately."

Gina only half heard him. She wandered from one wonderful room to the other, marveling at rich, carved woodwork, high ceilings, deep window seats, fireplaces everywhere and dilapidated though heartwarming charm her father's elegant home in Beverly Hills would never have.

"I love it!" she said sincerely, imagining the fun she could have restoring it. She turned to him under the dusty chandelier in the small library that looked out onto the crescent porch. "I'll do it over for you in my spare time. I can get everything at a good price, and Bobbi could handle all the reupholstering. That is, if you want it done over."

"Well, of course." He looked pleasantly surprised. "I expected you to hate it."

Her eyes widened. "Whatever for?"

He glanced around the room with its ancient, well-worn furnishings. "Well, it's hardly what you're used to."

She frowned and folded her arms. "I thought we'd already decided to abandon all preconceived notions about each other. I'm spoiled, but I can appreciate beauty. And you're a strong and tough man, but you have the heart of a teddy bear. Could we not forget that?"

He winced. "Teddy bear. I *will* forget that, if you don't mind. It doesn't suit my image of myself at all. And if any of my old corps buddies heard you say that, they'd laugh you off the planet."

She patted his cheek and said with playful drama, "I'm your wife, remember? I know things about you others will never see." She glanced at her watch. "It's after one. I suppose you're anxious to get to the hotel and back to work. Should I fix us some lunch first?" She wandered toward the kitchen, asking over her shoulder, "Is there anything in the refrigerator?"

He grabbed his jacket off the back of the sofa where he'd left it when they'd come inside. "I'll get something in the coffee shop on my way in. Call room service and they'll bring you whatever you want."

"I'll pick up groceries this afternoon then. Where shall I . . . ?"

He shook his head. "You don't leave the grounds without me, remember? Meet me in my office for dinner, I'll show you around the hotel, then tomorrow I'll have someone from security take you shopping."

She made a grim little face. "I keep forgetting. We've reached our destination, but the chase isn't over."

He cupped her chin in his hand and asked gently, "Is it starting to get to you?"

She sighed, catching his wrist and turning her lips into his palm. "No. At least I'm not in it alone anymore."

He pulled her to him and kissed her temple. "As long as you're on hotel grounds, you can pretend it doesn't exist, because there'll be someone to handle it for you." He pulled her away and smiled. "Try to relax this afternoon. It's been a rough week for you. Take a bath, read a book, order a giant lunch. After all..." He grinned. "You haven't eaten since we stopped for coffee in Cannon Beach and that was forty-five minutes ago."

Gina walked him to the door. "Keep it up, Gallagher, and you'll find out how difficult I can be."

He feigned a regretful look. "Then I'd have to show you how difficult *I* can be, and where would that get us? I think we should continue the team spirit we developed on the road."

She couldn't help the wicked grin that curved her lips. "Disagree most of the day and settle all arguments in the shower or the bathtub?"

"Or the hayloft," he added, leaning down to give her a parting kiss. "Unfortunately we don't have one here. Come on down about six."

She took a few steps out with him onto the porch. "You know, I don't have a dress to wear to dinner."

"This is the Oregon coast," he said. "Nothing takes second place to comfort. In our dining room you'll see casual and fancy dress." His gaze went to her hair, and the expression on his face accelerated her pulse. "Wear your hair up. It always makes you look like a queen, especially when you're naked."

AFTER PATRICK LEFT, Gina decided to take another tour and followed the overgrown stone path that led her through a corridor of mountain ash to the garden behind the hotel's central building. Sunny forsythia was in bloom, and white spirea, sweet-smelling lilac and hardy rhododendron. She walked slowly through it, inhaling the fragrances as they mingled with the wonderful but very cold river-fresh air. Tempting aromas also wafted out from the kitchen. She could hear the mild commotion of shouted orders, banging pots and pans and laughter.

She found herself hurrying as she walked around the building to go in through the front door and stopped just inside the hotel's lobby, gasping at its Victorian elegance. A dark oriental carpet brought out the warmth of the oak desk that took up one end of the enormous area. There were rose velvet draperies over delicate sheers and round oak tables and captain's chairs where people sat over drinks and conversation and watched the comings and goings in the lobby.

A subtle pink-and-green striped wallpaper rose up to the second level where she could see a gallery with more tables and books and magazines. Thriving fan palms stood near columns and in corners, and quiet music came from a trio near the lounge area.

Gina half expected to see the company of some Victorian drama, laughing and waving fans as they trooped out to a waiting carriage.

Instead a pretty young woman in a Victorian lace blouse and skirt came from behind the desk to greet her. "Mrs. Gallagher?"

"Yes." She couldn't help the little thrill she felt admitting it.

"I'm Katey. Mr. Gallagher asked me to watch for you." Petite and very blond, she leaned toward her conspiratorially. "We're all *so* happy for both of you."

Gina smiled as the young woman led her down a carpeted hallway toward an oak door at the end.

"When Mr. Gallagher came back to take over the hotel and moved into the old house," Katey whispered, "we could see him from Polly Dutton's window, looking out at the river. We were hoping he didn't end up like her, alone and lonely in that big old place."

"Who's Polly Dutton?" Gina asked.

"The Duttons founded Candle Bay," Katey explained. "Only it wasn't called Candle Bay then, it was just called Dutton. Anyway, Polly was supposed to marry a fisherman her father didn't approve of, only he was lost on the river. They never recovered his body. Polly kept a candle lit on her bedroom window every night for the rest of her life, on the chance that he was out there somewhere and needed a light to help him find his way home." She put both hands to her heart. "Isn't that romantic? That's how this became Candle Bay."

"So the house was here before the hotel?"

Katey nodded as she rapped on the door. "The first Mr. Gallagher added the Queen Anne porch to match his hotel. But Polly Dutton's father built the house."

A voice beyond the door shouted, "In!"

Katey opened the door for Gina. Patrick sat behind a large desk, his feet propped on a corner of it as he spoke on the phone. He'd apparently showered and changed when he got to work because he now wore a three-piece suit and wing tips. Behind him was a breathtaking view of the bay and the rest of the hotel complex. He waved Katey a thank-you and pointed Gina to the chair near him.

"Right," he was saying. "You'll pick up Bobbi, then?" There was a moment's pause. "Great. Gina's anxious to talk to her about helping decorate the house. It won't be ready for guests yet, but I'll put you two up in the hotel." He listened a moment and shook his head, absently studying an open book in his lap. "No, we're both fine. Just look into those few things for me, will you? Right. Thanks. No, I'll tell you more about that when you come up. No. Sorry. It's a long story, and I'm sure Gina will want to add a few things, and she'll want Bobbi to hear. Okay. Take care."

Patrick hung up the phone, leaned back in his chair and studied Gina in her new blue turtleneck and jeans and his ever-present leather jacket. She'd caught her hair up in a simple knot as he'd suggested, long bangs and dark tendrils framing her face.

He'd missed her this afternoon, and he'd felt the change in himself when she walked into his office. He'd worked like a fiend all afternoon. He'd written a check to Sin, who'd promised to send a check from his account to the motel owner in Santa Cruz and to the automobile dealer in Rockport. That would cover the bus he'd decided to keep and have the truck stored until it could be picked up. He knew Danforth and Gardner could certainly find him with some investigating, but he wasn't leaving any easy clues.

Patrick gave a long stretch and rotated his taut shoulders.

"How's Sin?" she asked.

He nodded. "Good. He says hi."

Her smile of anticipation filled him with a warm glow. "I can't wait to show Bobbi the house. She's going to love it. I spent all afternoon making plans."

"Did you order a feast from room service?"

She looked vaguely sheepish. "I skipped lunch."

"What?" Patrick brought his feet to the floor and studied her with exaggerated surprise. "You haven't had anything since mid-morning?" He glanced at his watch. "Almost eight hours? Are you feeling faint?"

She rolled her eyes at his teasing. "I got involved with floor plans and color schemes. I've been known to go into a trance at work and miss a meal or two."

"Horrors." He picked up the phone and jabbed a button. "And work gets done anyway without emergency runs for potato chips? Hi, Brian. Mrs. Gallagher and I will be in the restaurant. Then we're taking a tour of the hotel. I'll call again before we go home."

He cradled the receiver, stood and held a hand out for Gina's. "Come on," he said. "Let's get some food in you before your system fails."

The dining room was another model of turn-of-the-century elegance. Oak woodwork and gilded mirrors shone like jewels, snowy tablecloths were adorned with small pots of fresh flowers, and waiters and waitresses were dressed appropriately for the period.

The hostess led them to a table in the corner with a view of the bay and brightly lit Astoria on the other side. Gina drank in the beautiful sight for a moment, then turned to Patrick with a smile.

"I haven't seen you in a suit since our wedding," she said.

"That was only five days ago."

A waitress immediately filled their goblets with icy water and someone else brought an elegant silver pot of coffee. It smelled freshly ground and brewed.

"Seems like an eternity, doesn't it?" she asked, when they were alone again.

He shook his head, his eyes roving her face, feature by feature. "No," he replied softly. "Just a comfortably long time."

She sighed, ensnared by his warm gaze, marveling at the generous Fates that had crossed Patrick's path with hers. "That's what I meant," she amended in a whisper.

He handed her one of the menus the hostess had placed in the middle of the table. He ordered champagne and salmon with new potatoes and fresh asparagus.

They ate while companionably discussing her plans for redecorating the house. When they'd finished, Patrick took her on a tour of the hotel complex.

Gina zipped her jacket as they surveyed the construction of the new building. The night was now cold and spitting rain as they followed the recently refurbished rows of rooms to the water and inspected the empty boathouse.

It was dark inside and water lapped comfortingly along its middle, open to the water, where small boats had once been sheltered. "It's a shame you can't use it anymore," Gina said, looking at its octagonal leaded-glass windows and the old table and chairs in a corner that had never been removed. "What a charming building."

"I think it does get used," Patrick said, a smile in his voice as he came up behind her in the dark. "They think I don't know it, but there's a few romantic pairs on staff who come here during breaks and . . . do what lovers do.''

Gina turned in his arms and raised her hands to his face. "You mean this?" she asked, raising on tiptoe to kiss his lips. He leaned down slightly to accommodate her, his mouth warm and pliant.

"Mmm," he said, cupping the back of her neck in one hand. "Maybe we could arrange to use this place, too."

She nipped at his lip. "Maybe. But I'm not giving up my lunch break for it."

He tugged at a tendril of hair until she yelped. "You mean you only skip lunch for your work?"

"I do sometimes forget food when I'm really distracted."

He fell for the taunt, nibbling kisses along her parted lips, drawing away when she tried to share the kiss. Determined to provide her with a distraction she wouldn't soon forget, he nipped along her jaw to her ear, then flicked his tongue into it until she hunched her shoulder and gasped.

"Patrick . . ."

"Shh," he said, nibbling along her throat as he held her to him with one hand and unzipped and removed the leather jacket with the other.

"My . . . jacket . . ." she complained in breathless distraction, her head thrown back.

He pulled up the hem of the turtleneck she wore as he backed her into the dark shadows of the boathouse.

"Whose jacket?" he asked, closing a hand over her breast. He caressed it, rolling his thumb over the taut tip until she uttered a ragged little moan.

"What time do you have lunch tomorrow?" she asked.

"One," he replied.

"I'll be here."

"I can't hold out until tomorrow," he said, tracing her ear with the tip of his tongue. She hunched a shoulder as it tickled, gooseflesh rising on every inch of her body. He was driving her backward into the darkest corner of the boathouse.

"What...what if one of the other couples... comes?" She tried desperately to keep a grip on sanity as his mouth replaced the hand that had taunted her breast.

"It's the dinner shift," he replied after a moment. "No breaks for another hour."

"But, where...?"

There was a small cruiser moored deep inside that she hadn't been able to see in the darkness. He leapt aboard, reached out to catch her as she followed and led her inside where it was even darker.

"I can't see a thing," she whispered as he turned her, flattened a hand at her back and eased her backward onto a narrow bunk. He tossed her jacket and turtleneck onto the floor and laughed softly. "We don't have to see. This exercise merely requires touch."

Then she felt his mouth on hers and his fingers at the snap of her jeans. He straightened and reached both hands inside to tug her jeans and panties down. Her body stilled and she felt the heart of her go liquid as his fingertips slid over the swell of her bottom, down her thighs to the back of her knees. He threw her clothes aside, then cast his slacks and briefs with them. They came together immediately, explosively, without time or need to prepare.

Nothing existed for her but that moment on the narrow little cot, the weight of Patrick's body and the spicy scent of him, the delicious delight he brought her to in less time than it took her to breath his name.

Then the mad spiral began, spinning her, moving her hips into its tightening pattern until that shimmering little dot of promised pleasure became the focus of her whole world. She cried his name as it flew apart.

Patrick marveled, as he had every time he made love to her, at the utter perfection of being drawn in and embraced by her. But tonight there was a special magic. Tonight they weren't running. Tonight they were home—and nothing had changed. It amazed him.

As she trembled in his arms, he drove her higher and higher, spurred by her desperate little whispers of his name. The gentle bobbing of the boat helped him take both of them beyond anything even he'd known. He abandoned all control at the same moment she did, and he clung to her, feeling her arms around him tighten as the sensation of a mutual climax rushed along both of them like a free-fall through the night.

Patrick was the first to hear the giggle. They lay lazily entangled, Gina sprawled over him on the narrow bunk. "Uh-oh," he whispered.

Her head snapped up, her hair tumbled in her face. "What?"

He put a hand over her mouth. "Company," he said in an undertone. "Just be still."

"Be still?" she pulled his hand down, her body tense. "We're naked!"

"Not completely," he replied calmly. "Shh!"

"Not completely, but where it counts! If we..."

He pulled her head down until her mouth was pressed to his rocklike pectoral muscle. Snatches of conversation drifted into the boat.

"No, I was foolish to get serious about a medical student." It was Katey's voice. "You'll have years of school before you say we can get married. Then there's residency, and if you don't want children until you establish a practice, I'll be too old to have them!"

An earnest male voice said, "We'll have them, but when we can afford them. When it's more convenient."

"Convenient." Katey snickered. "Nothing's ever convenient. Life is never perfect. Except maybe for Mr. and Mrs. Gallagher." There was a dreamy sigh. "Have you seen them together?"

"I thought we came here to talk about us."

"She's beautiful, and he looks at her like she just fell from heaven." Another sigh. "I'll bet *they* have babies right away."

Gina bit the sturdy muscle under her lips. Patrick pinched her hip in retaliation, then covered her yelp with his other hand.

"Katey, come on," the young man pleaded. "If I owned all this, I'd be able to afford babies, too. We've wasted five minutes already. Do you want me to show you how I feel or not?"

"How you feel as a man who needs a woman? Or how you feel about you and me?"

Gina nodded, as though she approved of Katey's tactics. Patrick looked heavenward.

"It's all the same."

"No, it's not."

"You want to kiss me and hold me because it gives you pleasure, not because I'm important to you."

The male voice became skeptical. "Like it doesn't give you any pleasure. Like you just don't care when I..." His voice trailed away as he apparently chose deed over words. There was a satisfied sigh then a dreamy one.

"All right, I do like it when you love me. But I don't want five or six years before this goes any further."

There was a long, thick silence. Gina and Patrick frowned, both waiting.

"Well, I can't marry you right now, Katey," the male voice said. "It wouldn't be fair of me."

Another silence, then Katey's voice, high and a little shaky said, "Then it wouldn't be . . . fair of me to go on seeing you."

"Katey!"

There was the sound of tears and running footsteps, then an abrupt silence.

Patrick and Gina lay together for a long moment, staring at each other. Then Gina propped herself up on her forearms and looked sadly in the direction the footsteps had taken.

"Couldn't you give him a raise?" she asked. "So he could support a family while he's going to school, too?"

He smiled and brushed her hair back. "The inn already pays better than other hotels. The kids have to find a way to work it out."

Gina's gray eyes coaxed him. "Come on. There must be something you could do. Katey thinks you're a demigod."

He grinned. "Only demi? And what do *you* think?"

Gina leaned her chin on her folded hands. *I think I love you* was on the tip of her tongue, but she wasn't sure he was ready to hear it.

"I think we should restore this boat and sail it to Mexico when we go in February." Then she kissed his clavicle and began a slow, breathy path down his chest.

Patrick's breath caught in his throat as she reached her objective.

"Olé," he groaned.

Chapter Eleven

There were teddy bears suspended from heart-shaped balloons, dinosaurs riding bicycles, whimsical animals of all kinds having tea parties. Patrick studied the brightly colored wallpaper Gina held up and had to smile at it.

They stood in the middle of the room he'd first shown her three weeks before—the basement of the main building. It had once stored extra tables and chairs for the meeting rooms, but was now painted in the primary colors that predominated in the wallpaper.

Gina, dressed in dull gray sweats, swept a hand along one of the walls. "We'll have cribs and playpens here, and mats and pillows for sitting. Over there..." She pointed across the room, grabbed him by the wrist with one small, paint-spattered hand and tugged him with her. "We'll have stuff for the bigger kids, a comfy old sofa and a few decrepit chairs I found in your storage...." She added in an aside, "Bobbi can help me reupholster those when she comes. On that wall..." She pointed behind them. "We'll have all the cubbyholes where the kids can put their things, and that wall..." She walked to the front, still pulling him along. "I'll put half wipe-off boards and half bulletin boards. What do you think?"

He thought she was wonderful. In the paint-smeared sweats, with her hair pulled up and covered with his camouflage fatigue hat, she still made his heart beat like a jackhammer.

He couldn't believe how his perception of Gina had changed in the brief month they'd been married. He couldn't believe how his perception of *himself* had changed. The solitude he'd once valued had ceased to be a priority. He was now consumed with thoughts of their togetherness—memories they shared, plans for their future.

"I think it's great," he said, putting an arm around her and squeezing her to him. "Even better than I'd imagined. I appreciate how wholeheartedly you've attacked this project."

Her arms around his waist, she looked up at him, the brim of his hat shading her eyes against the fluorescent light. "You think you're the only one who feels tied to promises without a signature?"

They'd been so happy together that by some unspoken mutual agreement, they never mentioned that it wasn't forever. He was in so deep now, he even tended to forget.

They walked up the dark path home, arm in arm, Gina leaning against him, the light left on in their bedroom beckoning them home.

PATRICK TURNED his key in the lock and pushed the front door open. A spicy aroma wafted out to greet them.

He took an appreciative whiff as he closed and locked the door. "What is that?" he asked as he followed Gina toward the kitchen. "Gingerbread," she replied over her shoulder, tugging off the old sweater he had lent her to put over the sweats. "I ran home this afternoon to bake it so we could have it with our coffee when we came home. Brandied whipped cream or ice-cream topping?"

He put both arms around her when she stopped at the counter and nibbled at her neck. "You are *such* a domestic bargain. You wield a deadly curling iron, and you can bake, too. Sometimes I can't believe my good fortune. I'm going to be a very curly, very fat husband."

She giggled, taking a fistful of his hair to stop his nibbling and to allow herself to plant a kiss on his cheek. "I'll still love you, don't worry."

His eyes were an inch from hers, suddenly dark and intense. "You promise?"

Her eyes softened to gray velvet and her laughter gentled into a loving smile. "I promise," she whispered back.

He leaned an inch forward and kissed her with passion and tenderness and all the emotions growing between them he didn't completely understand yet. And with a promise for later.

He finally freed her and straightened. "Whipped cream," he replied to her previous question, his voice rusty and quiet. He turned to leave the kitchen. "I'll build a fire in the bedroom while you're fixing coffee. We can have it up there." He paused at the door to grin at her. "Okay?"

"Okay," she agreed.

Though the enormous old bedroom on the river end of the house was still desperately in need of fresh paint and new wallpaper, Gina had bought a new bedspread and curtains in burgundy and green, and they'd picked up an old love seat at a second-hand store in Astoria. She'd placed a matching green throw over it that she'd found in the attic. He'd come to love this room.

He built the fire and placed the kindling, then stood to reach to the broad mantel for a match. His eyes fell on Gina's Renaissance lovers lamp that had urged them home, and he found himself smiling again. The tulip light glowed brightly and had become Gina's tribute to Polly Dutton.

Patrick took a moment to lean his elbows on either side of the lamp and study it. He remembered how he'd seen it for the first time in the beam of a flashlight in a deserted barn. He'd thought it gaudy then, even foolish.

Now he saw it in a different light.

"No pun intended," he told himself, batting with a fingertip one of the sparkling crystals that hung from the tulip cup. It dangled and shone crazily, as bright as the lovers' smiles.

"I thought you were building a fire?" Gina asked, shouldering her way into the room with a tray bearing their late snack. "Do I have to do everything?" she teased, placing the tray on the small table in front of the love seat and coming around it to the fireplace.

She thought much later that she should have been suspicious of his grin. He stood directly in front of the fireplace, hands loosely on his hips, his eyes blazing with a passion that had grown even since the momentous decision made in the kitchen.

"*You* build the fire," he challenged. "I dare you."

His suggestive double entendre wasn't lost on her. Eager to accept the challenge, she unbuttoned the top button of his shirt and put her lips to the warm, muscular flesh there. "Your whipped cream will melt," she warned, unfastening the second and third buttons and kissing her way down the open vee.

He inched up her sweatshirt and coaxed her backward toward the bed. He dipped his index finger into the cream as they passed the coffee table.

Gina sank into the mattress, Patrick kneeling over her, and she felt his finger touch the cool cream just beneath her bra and trace a line down to the waistband of her panties.

Everything inside her shuddered as he nibbled up the cream.

"The gingerbread can't be this delicious," he said, reaching under her to unhook her bra, then toss it aside. "But I'll have to have another taste to be sure."

"WE'D PROMISED a garden-view suite to the Websters," Brian Scott, the Candle Bay Inn's night manager said anxiously to Patrick as he walked into the office with the morning paper. "But they're due in an hour and there isn't one free. The plumber's still working on the stopped-up sink in the south suite, the couple in the middle suite extended their stay by two days because they just *love* the north coast . . ." A roll of his eyes said he wasn't particularly crazy about it himself at the moment. Patrick's hardworking employee was the young man who'd been with Katey in the boathouse the night he and Gina had almost been discovered. "And the north suite is occupied as scheduled."

Patrick nodded from behind his desk. "Do we have a river-view suite free?"

Brian frowned. "Yeah, but it's forty dollars a night more."

"Let them have it for the same price. Explain that the guests in the room they were supposed to have are enjoying their stay with us so much, they've extended, and that we hope the same happens with them."

Brian visibly relaxed. "Right," he said and turned away.

Patrick opened the paper, his attention immediately arrested by the headline. Coastal Hotel Burns. He frowned over the three-column photo of a fire licking at the familiar pointed roof of a hotel just down the coast. He began to read the story.

"Mr. Gallagher!" A breathless Katey stood in his doorway.

Patrick looked up, bracing himself for yet another crisis, grateful, at least, that he wasn't in the Indian Beach Hotel owner's shoes.

"I have the president of the Northcoast Antique Dealers on the phone." She gulped a breath and shook her head. "He wants to know if we can host their annual meeting Memorial Day weekend. They'd booked the Indian Beach..." She indicated the newspaper open on his desk. "I could have buzzed you, but I wanted to make sure you'd read what happened."

He nodded. "Just reading it. How's the register look?"

"All the meeting rooms are free," Katey told him. "And he understands that their rooms would be scattered because it's so last-minute."

While grateful for her efficiency, he was torn between the bonus of having the hotel filled to capacity and the absolute havoc a last-minute booking that size would cause for him and his staff—particularly on the party weekend. But he already understood that the principle in commerce was "never turn down business or money."

He picked up the receiver, punched the blinking light, and made the frantic president of the North-coast Antique Dealers a very happy man.

RAIN DROVE at the kitchen windows as Gina packed a picnic basket. The idea was crazy, but then, it hadn't been sanity that had put this marriage together.

She had promised to stay out of Patrick's way, but it was harder than she'd imagined.

Since he'd booked the antique dealers' convention, he'd worked long hours checking details and fielding the scores of crises that came up daily with so much construction and remodeling going on while the hotel remained open to guests.

She hadn't had a meal with him in days. They'd had little time to talk. She was determined to change that.

She picked up the wall phone and pushed the button that dialed his office.

"Gallagher," he said. He sounded preoccupied and she could hear the shuffle of papers.

"Hi," she said brightly. "I'm calling to announce that the center's ready for children. I put the last piece of furniture in place myself this morning."

"Terrific!" he praised, sounding enthused but still distracted. "I'll run by on my way home."

"I packed a lunch," she said. "I thought I could take you on a tour on your break, then we could drive to the lookout and eat."

"Sorry, Gina." He did sound apologetic, but still distracted. The tone reminded her of her father. "I've got a plumber here for a problem, and a shipment of red napkins is lost."

She hesitated a moment. "The dining room is oak and green and white."

"Exactly."

She sighed. "You can't spare twenty minutes to eat?"

"Not this afternoon. Why don't you come down to the coffee shop for lunch? Katey's there."

She huffed impatiently, determined to get through to him. "I don't miss Katey, I miss *you.*"

DOWN THE SLOPE, in the proprietor's office in the main building of the Candle Bay Inn, Patrick heard Gina's words and for a moment was lost for a reply.

He'd been afraid this would happen. Sometimes, down in the depths of his soul, he admitted there'd been times when he'd been afraid it *wouldn't* happen. But that was confusing, and he liked things plain and simple.

"I told you the day you proposed this marriage," he said reasonably, "that I work long hours."

"I know," she countered blandly. "And the first time I complained you would send me back to my father by fourth-class mail."

There was a long pause. She waited for him to say he hadn't meant it. He didn't.

He waited for her to say she'd never want to leave—
ever. She didn't.

So Patrick did what years of military training had
taught him. He attacked while the opportunity was
his.

"Do I have to buy stamps or what?" he asked.

Gina was hurt for just a moment. She let herself
compare him to her father and remembered all the
times Wyatt Raleigh's work had taken precedence over
her needs.

Then she remembered that as a child, she'd been
powerless to change that. She was a woman now—a
smart one.

She drew a breath and said evenly, "Forget the
stamps. Save your money and buy a hard hat. You're
going to need it before I'm finished with you."

Patrick stared at the receiver for a moment after the
line went dead. Then he cradled it, not sure whether to
laugh or worry.

PATRICK LOOKED UP at a complex arrangement of
dripping pipes in the basement of the main building
while the plumber explained that a large part of it had
to be replaced.

"It was quality work," the man said, "but it's very
old. I'd suggest—"

"Mr. Gallagher!" A bellman wound his way between the drips and handed him a cordless phone. "A
problem at the desk."

He'd done something to offend the Fates today, Patrick thought as he pressed the Phone button.

"Mr. Gallagher," Katey said anxiously. "There's a problem in 209 and the guest wants to see the manager. Brian isn't here yet."

He frowned. "What kind of problem?"

"I don't know. The implication was that I'm too much of an underling to discuss it with."

Oh, good. An unhappy guest with a Caesar complex. Just what he needed to round out his day. "On my way," he said.

He handed the phone back to the bellman, told the plumber to do what had to be done and took the elevator to the second floor. He tried to adjust his attitude on the brief ride up.

He'd been thinking about Gina since she'd hung up on him two hours before. His brain told him he had no reason to feel guilty, but his heart longed to chuck aside the rest of the day's responsibilities and go to her. He'd find a way to make it up to her after the big weekend.

The elevator doors parted and he stepped out onto the soft blue carpet. He rapped on the door of 209.

"Come in," a faint feminine voice shouted.

Patrick stepped into what seemed to be an empty room. It appeared in perfect order, the softly shaded nautical decor spotless and fresh.

"Hello?" he called.

"Yes?" a slightly louder voice replied.

"It's the manager," he called back. "I understand there's a problem."

"It's in here!" the voice called back.

It came from somewhere inside the dressing-room arch. He studied the shadows there in mild concern, reluctant to venture farther.

He stopped to lean against the molding. "Something wrong with the shower?" he asked.

"No, the bed," the voice replied silkily.

He turned to look at it. Then something yanked his tie and turned him back. He found himself face-to-face with Gina—naked.

A flare of annoyance warred with an eruption of hormones.

"And what precisely," he asked, "is wrong with it?"

She pressed herself against him and bit his chin. "You aren't *in* it."

"Gina..." he said in laughing protest, trying to disengage her hands as she unknotted his tie. "I told you I can't..."

The words died on his lips as her bent knee rubbed along the inside of his thigh. His resistance went down and his blood pressure went up—and it wasn't alone.

His tie was off and she was working on the buttons of his shirt.

"I know," she said, planting a kiss on the jut of his ribs. "You don't have time. But I knew you'd make time for a guest. I've booked the room."

He took a handful of her hair, prepared to pull her away and explain the complete attention to detail required to keep the inn running smoothly, to tell her that she was being childish and demanding.

Then she lifted her eyes to him. They were large and soft and filled with love, and he knew she hadn't been motivated by selfishness.

Every other thought fled in his mind. There would be a time to deal with them. He nobly decided to let her have her way.

She tugged the shirt and jacket off. As she hung them on the hanger just inside the dressing room, he stepped out of his slacks and briefs and tossed them over the luggage rack.

She crooked a finger at him. "Follow me," she said, turning to the bed.

He reached out and pulled her back, lifting her into his arms and tucking her legs around his waist.

"I don't follow," he said softly, covering her mouth with a deep, drugging kiss. "I was taught to lead. But I'll take you there."

His arms were crossed to support her, a hand cupping each hip. She wriggled closer, wondering if anything in the world ever felt as right as the warm, naked flesh of the one you loved against your own.

"Then do," she whispered, kissing him back.

He leaned over the bed to drop her in the middle, but she kept a grip on him and tugged so that he fell with her, then she rolled him over and knelt astride him. She braced her hands on his shoulders and looked down into his dark eyes, heavy lidded with anticipation, yet soft with amusement.

"I was never an officer," she said, tracing a line from between his pecs to his navel with the tip of her fingernail. "But, I've always been my own boss. *I* invited *you* here. We do this my way."

"I think *tricked me here* is the term," he said, his fingertips roaming up her sides and circling her breasts. "But do go on. I'm more than happy to cooperate."

"Good." She began to kiss a trail across his chest, then down his torso. She scooted backward to kiss and nibble over his hipbone and down his thighs, ignoring that part of him straining for her touch.

He groaned. "Little witch!"

She started back up again, making him mindless with taunting forays that led everywhere but where he wanted her most.

"Gina," he finally pleaded huskily, "have a heart!"

She poised over him. He took hold of her waist and assumed control, entering her with one smooth but desperate thrust. "I do," she whispered as they began to move together, swaying in opposing directions to make the ultimate circle, the quintessential yin and yang of life. "And it beats for you."

Pleasure erupted with a power that awed him. And he knew it wasn't merely because of Gina's ardent ministrations, but because of the love he felt for her.

She whispered a high-pitched little cry and collapsed on top of him.

"See," she said after a moment. "Don't I beat the traditional lunch at your desk? I've got a picnic basket in the closet and—" She tried to push herself up to go and get them.

But Patrick wrapped his arms around her and rolled them over. She blinked up at him in surprise, then raised her wrist to look at her watch.

He began to do to her what she'd done to him.

"Patrick, we've already used half your lunch—" She broke off to gasp feelingly, "Oh, my! Oh, Patrick, I don't think I could take another. Ooooooh!"

"You weren't very merciful with me a few minutes ago."

"I thought you needed to slow down, to..."

She arched up in his arms and he felt her body shudder with the pleasure he'd given her. He entered her again and took her possessively, completely, deliciously.

NAKED, Gina peered into the picnic basket she'd earlier brought to the chair beside the bed. Leaning against the propped-up pillow, the blankets drawn up to his waist, Patrick smiled and enjoyed the view.

"An orange?" she asked, glancing at him over her shoulder. "Or an oatmeal cookie?"

He raised an eyebrow. "Since when does the kitchen have oatmeal cookies?"

Taking that for assent, she grabbed the baggy of cookies and crawled back into bed. Patrick lifted the blanket for her and pulled her into his arm.

"I baked them last night while you were working," she said, putting one between his lips.

His strong even teeth snapped off a bite. He made a sound of approval as he chewed. "I'm glad to see," he said finally, "that you were usefully occupied. The chicken and salad were also wonderful. This lunch was an inspired idea."

She nibbled delicately at the rest of the cookie. "I just didn't want you to think I'd put up with that forever."

He reached past her to the bedside table for the glass of wine they were sharing. "Put up with what?"

"Being last on your list of priorities because you're afraid to face the fact that you need me."

He looked at her in surprise. "Of course I need you," he said. "I thought I'd made that more than clear."

He offered her the glass. She took a sip and handed it back. "I mean in ways that aren't physical." Their faces were so close that she could see the gold flecks in the depths of his brown eyes. She looked deeply into them, desperate to read there what he truly felt. "I came to this room because I knew I could get your attention this way." She sighed in self-deprecation. "And because I feel as though my life starts all over every time you love me. But I want you to know I won't settle for just this."

She took her courage in both hands and admitted candidly, "I don't think I'll be able to leave you in March, Patrick."

He put the wine aside and enfolded her in his arms. "That's good," he said, "I'd hate to have to chase you down."

He wasn't quite getting the point. "*Why* don't you want me to leave, Patrick? Because we're so good in bed, because there's someone in the house when you come home? Don't you want to share more with me?"

He wanted to tell her it was because he loved her and wasn't sure he could live without her, but he'd been a soldier too long. The most important lesson he'd learned was that vulnerability meant defeat.

"Because you're mine," he said, holding her to him. "And it still isn't safe for you out there. The fact that whoever's after you hasn't appeared, doesn't mean he isn't out there waiting."

"Patrick..."

The phone rang shrilly. Patrick reached for it. "Yes?" He listened a moment. "Yes, Katey." He cast a scolding glance at Gina. "No, that's all right. I'll be there in fifteen minutes. And you and I have to have a talk, young lady, on where your loyalties lie."

Gina heard but couldn't decipher Katey's reply.

Patrick looked at the receiver, then replaced it in the cradle.

"She said her loyalty lies with Polly Dutton." He frowned at Gina. "What in the hell does that mean?"

Gina laughed softly, settling for half a victory. He hadn't said he loved her, but he did say he wouldn't let her leave.

"I imagine," she said, pushing the blankets back, "I remind her of Polly. She, too, was always trying to lure her lover home with a light in the window."

He caught her arm and pulled her back against him when she would have gotten to her feet.

"You're going weird on me, my love," he said, kissing her temple. "Maybe you've been confined too long. I was going to send the hotel limo to the airport for Sin and Bobbi, but maybe we'd better pick them up."

The idea delighted her. It would be wonderful to have him to herself for the few hours it would take to drive to Portland and back.

"But can you leave the hotel with the big weekend starting tomorrow?"

"Wasn't that the point of this lesson?"

She grinned up at him. "You mean, you've learned it?"

He laughed softly. "I don't know. But I've sure as hell enjoyed it."

Chapter Twelve

"Oh, Bobbi!" Gina hugged her friend to her then held her away, drinking in the warm and robust look of her. She hadn't realized how much she needed a friend until that moment. "You look great! Just the same!"

Bobbi made a face. "It's only been five weeks. Did you expect me to have aged?"

Gina swatted her arm, then tucked hers into it. "Of course not. Come on. I can't wait to get you home and take you through our wonderful house."

Bobbi hesitated as Gina tried to lead the way. "The bags..."

"Oh, don't worry," Gina said, smiling over her shoulder at Patrick. "I brought the Candle Bay Inn's chief bellman with me."

As the women headed toward the parking lot arm in arm, Sin picked up Bobbi's large piece of soft-sided luggage and handed it to Patrick. "Well," he said, "I see marriage has really improved your status. From owner of the hotel to bellboy."

Patrick laughed and started to follow the women, then waited to give Sin a minute to catch up. "It's improved a lot of other things about my life."

Patrick took two steps back to his friend as Sin, holding his own large bag, tangled with a small, masculine-looking tote, a larger brocade one and a camera he was trying to loop on his shoulder. "What is your problem?" Patrick asked.

"You'd think she could carry her own camera," Sin said, casting a disgruntled look in Bobbi's direction.

Patrick took it from him. "That better?" he teased. "What's the matter? She hasn't fallen for you yet?"

Sin straightened and glowered, the expression half playful, half serious. "If you've invited me here to torment me, tell me right now and I'll turn right around...."

Patrick frowned at him worriedly. "Sin, you're losing your sense of humor. You want to talk about it?"

"No."

Patrick watched Sin march off after Gina and Bobbi, and grinned. Sin didn't have to explain what was bothering him. Patrick thought he knew.

"I'LL USE CORDOVAN leather," Bobbi said, running a hand over the torn upholstery of the library chairs. "Or maybe brocade? And I think Patrick should have a throne chair for that spot by the window." She pointed to the leaded-glass window that looked out onto the hotel. Now a threadbare upholstered chair sat there, a book on its arm.

Bobbi straightened, her arms wrapped around herself. "Gina, this place is a masterpiece! I'll make a list of everything before I go and I'll send you fabric swatches. I'll come back in August and spend my vacation doing the living room for you, then I'll ship whatever you decide on for the other stuff and you can have someone local do it. By this time next year, it'll be like something people pay money to tour."

Gina hugged her. "It's so good to see you. I wish the bedrooms were in better shape so you could stay here instead of the hotel."

"Oh, I'll be fine." Bobbi put an arm around Gina's shoulders and wandered with her back into the dining room. "So..." Her voice took on a careful quality as she dropped her arm and walked slowly around the round oak table, fingertips rubbing lightly over the smooth, burnished surface. "Things haven't worked out precisely the way you planned, have they?"

Gina's eyes widened with surprise. How could she know?

Bobbi smiled and slipped into a ladder-backed chair. She propped her elbow on the table and a chin on her hand. "You fell in love, didn't you?"

Gina sat two chairs away and nodded. "Deeply. Desperately. Unreservedly." She sighed and added, "Unfortunately."

Bobbi crossed one arm over the other and frowned. "Why? Patrick's wearing precisely the same look you're wearing. I'd say he fell in love, too."

Gina grimaced. "The point is, *he* won't say it."

"You know men." Bobbi sighed. "They're not always quick about these things. They haven't the vaguest idea what to do with a woman. Except the obvious, of course."

Gina stood, restlessly pacing around the table. "You think I should settle for being wanted instead of loved?"

Bobbi shook her head, obviously not requiring time to consider the question. "No. Don't ever settle. But bide your time. You have ten more months to this bargain, haven't you?"

Gina sighed and sank into a chair opposite her friend. "Yes. I guess I feel this way because his attitude is a lot like my father's was. He's always so busy...."

"Hey." Bobbi reached across to place her hand over Gina's. "Have a little faith. He stayed with you after he learned you'd tricked him, he kept you safe during that awful trip. I think you're so used to your father's remoteness that you don't recognize genuine busyness when you see it."

Gina had told Bobbi about their chase up the coast while they'd unpacked her things. She thought now that her memories of it weren't awful at all. Was she being paranoid and selfish?

"And he seems very attentive," Bobbi went on. "He'll come around. I'll bet you fifty bucks."

Gina laughed. "Fifty bucks? On my future?"

Bobbi shrugged. "Love's a dangerous game. The stakes don't matter as much as your courage to play."

"I APOLOGIZE if suggesting you bring Bobbi ruined your long weekend," Patrick said to Sin. They were testing a new forty-foot boat just purchased for the inn. Patrick handled the helm, while Sin leaned against the safety rail and stared quietly over the water.

Sin shook his head. "Nothing could ruin this place. She's just kind of . . . I don't know . . . cold. Remote. I hate that in a woman."

Patrick remembered their easy amity the day of his and Gina's wedding. "You two got along so well the day Gina and I got married. What happened?"

"Who knows?" Sin turned his face into the wind, then zipped his jacket up the last three inches. "I called her for a date and she turned me down. Coldly. So I guess I misread her." He turned back to Patrick as the wind tossed his short blond hair. "Isn't it ever going to warm up? It's Memorial Day weekend, for God's sake. Spring. Maybe you should have bought a ski lift for the inn instead of a boat for charter trips."

"Come on. You love your boat."

"It's a sailboat in sunny Southern California. Sailing in balmy waters isn't the same as sitting on deck in a survival suit waiting for something to nibble on your line.''

Patrick turned the boat in a wide circle and headed back for the inn's dock. ''You Southern Californians,'' he teased with a grin as Sin braced himself against the spray shield. ''Bunch of wimps. Any dude can wear shorts, lie in the sun and hold a sail line. It takes more guts and brains to go fishing here than it does to compete in the America's Cup down South.''

Sin groaned. ''And I suppose you have as many preposterous stories about the fish that get away, don't you?''

''Of course not.'' Patrick grinned. ''Nothing I go after gets away.'' He turned suddenly serious. ''You have a detective on staff with your firm, don't you?''

''Yeah. Jason Watters. You want him to look into the two guys who attacked you and Gina on the road?''

''No. I'd like to fax him our list of guests for the convention. Make sure everyone on it is who he says he is.''

''You have suspicions?''

''I don't know.'' Patrick hunched a shoulder. ''I have a house full of antique dealers. Could be coincidence, but I'd like to be sure.''

''Right. We'll do it the minute we get back.''

''YIKES,'' Bobbi said under her breath. ''It's like Times Square in here.''

Sin kept a hand on each woman's arm as they wound their way through the crowded lobby toward the main dining room. The antique dealers were registering, along with the regularly scheduled guests. The elegant lobby was thick with irregularly formed lines of people talking and laughing, checking touring brochures and getting acquainted.

Gina noted quite a few children in the group and thought the new day-care center might be full tomorrow.

"This looks good for Patrick," Sin said into Gina's ear as they cleared the worst of the crowd. "You two will be able to retire young, live and travel in the lap of luxury."

His casual remark made Gina turn instinctively to Bobbi with a questioning if not accusing look. Bobbi's expression told her she'd pay later for even thinking she'd shared her confidence.

The headwaiter seated them and gave Gina the message that Patrick was held up and would join them as quickly as he could.

Sin groaned dramatically. "Two women all to myself. Whatever shall I do?"

Bobbi smiled blandly at him and batted her lashes. "Take comfort in the fact that one of them has a jealous husband, who's just a little bigger than you, and the other has no interest in you whatsoever."

Sin returned Bobbi's bland look. "Thank you, Miss Perducci. I'm so glad I drove all the way from Malibu to Burbank to pick you up, made all your flight arrangements and carried your two-ton bag of makeup the three miles from the terminal to the car. Your gratitude, not to mention your good manners, are overwhelming."

"Guys..." Gina began placatingly.

Bobbi took Sin's bait. "Travel arrangements. You must have been on the phone for hours to arrange to have me seated next to a little boy who got Slimer String all over me, and to have had me served a vegetarian dinner that was specially planned for the person who was supposed to have my seat."

"Didn't I get you another lunch?"

"Who can eat," she demanded, "after one mouthful of lasagna made with eggplant instead of meat!"

"Bobbi—" Gina tried.

"You could have restrained yourself," Sin interrupted stiffly, "from pouring your cola on the stewardess."

"The little boy," Bobbi said, low in her throat, enunciating every word, "threw his drink at the stewardess when she gave him ginger ale instead of cola. Had you stuck around to see that my problem was taken care of, you'd have known that!"

"Bobbi? Sin, really..."

"You had just told me," Sin retorted, his color deepening, "that I was free to leave the plane. That you could handle it. Considering we were still at thirty thousand feet, I chose simply to return to my seat."

"Which was seven rows back from mine," Bobbi said, pointing a finger in the air. "If that doesn't prove that you wanted nothing to do with..."

People were beginning to turn their way.

"I'll just go see what's keeping Patrick," Gina said.

Sin and Bobbi, still battling, failed to notice that she was standing. She found the headwaiter, asking him to bring champagne to their table and to keep pouring, hoping to add a little effervescence to her friends' dispositions, and headed for Patrick's office.

She stopped halfway across the lobby when Katey beckoned her to the desk. The clerk held out her left hand with a giggle of delight. It sported a beautiful pearl flanked by diamond chips. Gina exclaimed at its beauty, but looked into Katey's eyes, unsure that it indicated what she suspected.

"We're engaged!" she bubbled. No champagne necessary there, Gina thought with a pleased smile. "We couldn't afford a diamond, but I think this pearl is the most beautiful ring I ever saw."

Gina leaned over the desk to hug her. "That's wonderful, Katey. Congratulations! What happened to change Brian's mind?"

Katey glanced surreptitiously left and right. "Mr. Gallagher."

Gina stared at her a moment. "What?"

"I'm not sure what happened exactly," Katey said, "but all I know is he went into Mr. Gallagher's office to talk about a problem at the desk, stayed quite a while, and that night he invited me to dinner and proposed. It was the same afternoon you booked the room." Katey beamed, apparently pleased to have been a conspirator in the little ruse that had gotten Patrick there.

Gina gave her another hug, surprised that Patrick had taken Katey's side. She thought cautiously that it could be a good sign. Maybe Bobbi was right. "That's terrific. Just goes to show you a good boss can fix anything."

Gina turned from the desk to go in search of Patrick and collided with an elegantly mustached gentleman in an overcoat and an Irish bog hat.

"Oh, my gosh!" She juggled the small square box she'd knocked from his grasp. She lost it once, caught it with less style than luck with her fingertips, watched it do a complete turn just above her head, then caught it against her with a gasp of surprise.

"Well done!" the man praised.

Gina held the box out, but he hesitated before taking it. She thought she saw recognition in his eyes for a moment, then he smiled, doffed his hat, took the box and said in a deep, rusty voice, "If you don't play for the Trailblazers, you should."

She shrugged a shoulder, liking the *Field and Stream* magazine-cover look of him. "I tried out," she said. "Too short. Have we met?"

He shook his head regretfully, extending his hand. "I wish I could take that line and run with it, unfortunately I'm due to host a welcome meeting in ten minutes and, as you can see . . ." He indicated the luggage at his feet and the fact that he hadn't checked in. "I'm hardly prepared. Ah, Miss . . . ?"

Gina placed her hand in his. "Mrs.," she corrected. "Gallagher. You're with the antique dealers?"

"I am."

"Well, let me get a . . ." She turned to call for a bellman and found one standing right behind her, along with Patrick, who'd apparently been watching her encounter.

He gave her one brief indeterminate glance, then extended his hand to their guest. "Welcome to Candle Bay. I'm your host, Patrick Gallagher. This is my wife, Gina."

The man grinned broadly and shook his hand. "Dan Porter. I own Newport Niceties. It was good of you to take our group at the last moment like this."

"It's our pleasure, of course." Patrick gestured to a second clerk just coming out of the office. "Would you register this gentleman, please?" He turned to the bellman. "After you've taken him to his room, please escort him to the Cormorant meeting room."

"Yes, sir."

Patrick smiled affably. "Enjoy your stay."

"I will, thank you." The man nodded politely to Gina. "Mrs. Gallagher."

She smiled over her shoulder as Patrick led her toward the dining room. "He was ni—" she began, smiling up at Patrick only to find he was frowning down at her.

"'Have we met?'" he quoted her question with a suggestion of mockery. "You didn't ask him what astrological sign he was, did you?"

She looked at him in surprise. Jealousy? Another good sign. She grinned. "Oh, we cut through all that. I'm meeting him later at the boathouse."

He stopped several yards from the dining room to look down into her eyes. His held a hint of ill temper.

She put conciliatory hands to his chest. "Really, Patrick. I bumped into him—literally—while I was on my way to look for you. Sin and Bobbi have done nothing but quarrel, and I was looking for a more amenable dinner companion." She raised an eyebrow. "You are going to be, aren't you?"

He ran a hand down his face and sighed wearily. "Maybe if I have a lobotomy. It's been a hell of a day."

"Come with me." She took his hand and pulled him with her to the back of the lobby, down a utility corridor and to a door marked Supplies. It was locked.

She smiled at him. "You have the key, haven't you?"

He was looking at her warily. "Yes, but..."

She leaned against the doorjamb, her pose indolent and suggestive. "My surgery tools are in there."

The ill temper slid away instantly to be replaced by lazy amusement. "Really." He handed her the key. "Show me."

She opened the door, flipped on the light and led the way inside. The space was narrow, crowded on both sides with front-desk and office supplies.

He reached to a pencil cup that held half a dozen stainless steel, no-frills letter openers. He tested the dull tip of one with his index finger. "You're not going to operate with this, I hope."

She took the opener from him, plopped it back in the cup and put her arms around his neck. "No cutting. I prescribe an oral medication."

His eyes ignited. She loved it when that happened. "Then dose me, Doc," he whispered, lowering his mouth to meet hers.

Every tedious, unmanageable detail of his day dissolved as she ministered to him. She toyed with his tongue, nibbled at his bottom lip, drank from him with a thirst that made him feel humble. Could she really need him that much? As much as he needed her?

"That better?" she asked, moving her lips along his jaw to his ear.

He groaned, wishing desperately that they were home.

"Almost," he said, injecting a pathetic quality into his tone.

"All right," she said, working little kisses back toward his lips. "One more application. We don't want you overdosing when Sin and Bobbi are still waiting for us."

"Just go back to the dining room and tell them I broke something—I swear I'm about to."

"They're your friends."

"I want my doctor."

"I'll be going home with you, remember?" She kissed him again, more deeply, more thirstily than before, then pulled away and drew a deep breath to restore herself.

Patrick took a handful of her hair and looked with mock severity into her eyes. "All right, but don't you dare order dessert."

Love and passion blazed in his eyes. They were hot, sincere, honest.

The sound of a key in the lock made them move apart and turn to opposite sides of the narrow little room. Katey walked in and stopped short with a little cry of surprise.

The airless room was now warm from their bodies and smelled of her perfume, his cologne, and the suggestion that they'd mingled.

"Looks okay to me," Gina said in a tone of cool efficiency. She held an open box out to Patrick. "What do you think?"

He gave the long forms the box held a deliberate scrutiny. "I think we should reorder. Three copies of this form aren't enough. I know they come in quadruplicate. Make a note of that." He turned to Katey with a calm smile. "Hi, Kate. Everything all right?"

She looked from her boss to his wife, apparently unsure which of the three of them should feel guilty. "Fine," she answered absently. "I needed another box of pens. You know how they're . . . always disappearing."

"Right." Patrick turned Gina to the door and pushed her through. "We'll leave you to it. We'll be in the dining room if you need me."

As the supply-room door stood open behind them, they heard Katey's voice say in obvious confusion, "Laundry tally forms in quadruplicate?"

Chapter Thirteen

"Now, when Hilton calls and tries to lure you away to handle his hotels in Europe," Gina teased, walking Patrick from the coffee shop, where they'd met Sin and Bobbi for breakfast, to his office, "don't act eager. Everything here is going so well, I'm sure you'll be able to name your price."

As they walked across the lobby, conventioneers with matching notebooks in hand hurried past in laughter and eager conversation. The man from Newport Niceties, in conversation with two other men, spotted Patrick and Gina and smiled and waved as he and his companions stepped onto an elevator.

Patrick put an arm around Gina's shoulders as they turned down the administrative corridor. "You want to see Europe?"

She stared a moment, surprised by his question. "No. I was teasing."

"Good. Because nothing's going to budge me from Candle Bay. I got to see the world in the corps, but

I've known I'd settle down here since I left to go to college." His gaze probed hers. "You're happy here."

His statement had a vaguely tentative quality—an unusual tone for him. He was always so sure of what he knew.

She parted her lips to assure him that she was happy, but she was concerned enough about how she would live without him if he couldn't come to love her that the words stalled in her throat.

Patrick saw her hesitation. Instantly the glow of success this weekend had built in him was snuffed as though someone had pulled a shade. He knew what she wanted to hear and was angry with himself for being unable to say it, and with her for making him feel that way.

Gina saw frustration and confusion in his expression, and the beginnings of temper.

"Patrick, we—"

"Mr. Gallagher, can you come to the Cormorant meeting room?" A bellman out of breath skidded to a stop beside them. "A guest fainted. We called 911, but we thought you should . . ."

Patrick hesitated only long enough to give Gina a stiff, quietly spoken, "We'll talk later," and headed off for the meeting room at a run, the bellman chasing after him.

PATRICK STOOD under the hot shower in the bathroom off his office and decided there were advantages to a foul mood he hadn't anticipated. People left you alone. He hadn't had a whole day of peace since he'd first taken over for his grandfather.

He dried off briskly, pulled on briefs and a T-shirt, then the tux he kept in his office.

He ran over the evening's details in his head, knowing all the various department heads would carry out their responsibilities with their customary style and efficiency. All he had to do was appear, looking successful and in control of everything to assure everyone that the young Gallagher ran the same fine house his grandfather had.

The news media would be there in force, and as far as he knew, every travel agent they'd invited had accepted.

The antique dealers' convention was going exceptionally well. Even the woman who'd fainted yesterday awoke laughing, refusing to be taken away in an ambulance. She'd insisted she'd fainted from too much good food and too much partying—she blamed the Candle Bay Inn for its great chef and hospitable atmosphere.

Patrick was startled to a stop when he walked out of the small bathroom into his office, yanking at the bow tie already strangling him, and found Gina staring out his window. The ballroom visible beyond the glass glittered like a crown in the darkness. Against the backdrop of brightly lit Astoria, it looked like a tiara that had slipped from some hidden treasure trove.

Gina also looked like part of the booty, in an electric blue dress woven with silver threads and beads.

The back was cut almost to her waist, and her hair was piled in a complicated twist. He studied her creamy skin and the enticing line of her neck with a familiar quickening in his gut.

Sensing his presence, she looked over her shoulder to give him a tentative smile. "Hi," she said softly, then turned back to the view. "It looks like something out of *Ali Baba,* doesn't it?"

He came to stand behind her, leaving a hairbreadth between them. Her fragrance wafted around him, making him feel as though he just might lose his head.

GINA HAD DRESSED for the festivities, determined to pretend to herself that she was loved.

"It does," he replied, unable to stop himself from putting a hand on her arm and stroking her silky skin. "Do you feel like Scheherazade?" He turned her to him, looking deeply into the same expression he'd seen that morning that had troubled him all day. She tried to hide it with a smile, but failed. He asked gently, "Or are you Aladdin with your unconventional lamp?"

She laughed and the sound ran over him like a balm. She took his hand in her two and began to lead him away.

"I have a thousand-and-one tales to tell you, O Sultan," she said.

At the door he flipped the office lights off and they stood together in the semidarkness of the empty administrative corridor. "There's only one story I'm interested in hearing," he warned softly. "I want you to tell me you're happy."

"I love you," she said softly, "but that's not quite the same thing, is it?" She tugged him toward the sounds of revelry already beginning in the dining room. "But now we feast and dance."

"HOWARD WANTED to go to Mexico, but I said, 'Howard, sunshine is so ordinary! I want to visit the Northwest. I want the power and passion of nature...'"

Patrick was absolutely sure that whatever Belinda Suffolk wanted she got. As he led her around the ballroom's dance floor, he wondered if he would have permanent handles where her stubby, bejeweled fingers had gripped him.

He looked longingly across the room to where Gina danced with Belinda's husband. She'd been claimed by one laughing male guest after another all evening, and he had yet to dance with her.

As he watched, Sin cut in on Howard and whisked Gina away. Patrick sighed, resigned to having to listen to more of Belinda's dramatic oratory.

"Where men are men and women still know how to respect them and get the most of their marital investment."

Patrick glanced down at Belinda. "Pardon me?"

"Well, marriage isn't all 'separate but equal,' you know," she said, giving him a slap on his shoulder that he was sure dented it. She smiled broadly. "I suppose being a newlywed, you don't know that, but you can't treat marriage like an integration of neighborhoods. It's more complicated than that. It's down and dirty. It's love. If you think you're going to get back exactly what you give, then you need to invest in safe stock, not another human being." She jabbed an index finger at him, making a hole in the dent she'd left previously. "Marriage takes both of you giving one hundred percent and taking up the slack when the other just doesn't have it to give. Next time it'll be your turn. That's what makes marriage work. Not being perfect, but knowing how to give."

Patrick felt a jab on his back. For a moment he thought Belinda had developed some form of rear attack, but he turned his head to discover Sin behind him, Gina in his arms.

"Change partners?" Sin suggested. To Belinda he said, "Howard told me you have a sailing story about snapping a mast off at Newport, Rhode Island, that'll curl my hair."

Preening at the invitation, arms still raised in dancing mode, Belinda sailed toward Sin like a racing sloop with its spinnaker set.

Patrick drew Gina into his arms. Happy laughter and the cheerful strains of a contemporary ballad filled the room as he fond a quiet corner and moved slowly with the music.

"It's after eleven," he said, "and I've yet to hear one of your stories. I'm afraid I'll have to take my scimitar to you at midnight."

Gina wrapped both arms around his neck and felt his arms tighten around her waist as he drew her closer. They touched from nose to knees, and a little anticipatory shudder ran through her.

Patrick felt her tremble and knew without a doubt it was futile to struggle any longer. She belonged to him, but in making that happen, he'd given himself to her. Independence be damned. He was in love.

He kissed her cheek and whispered into her ear, "Come on. We're going to disappear for a while."

Gina heard the urgency in the softly spoken statement and drew back to look into his eyes. They were dark and steady but turbulent.

Her heart gave an uncomfortable thud. Maybe she shouldn't have told him she loved him. It wasn't part of the deal. Was he about to declare it null and void?

"Where did you want to go?" she asked.

"The boathouse," he replied.

She suspected he wasn't taking her there to set sail for pleasure on the little cruiser.

He caught her wrist and led her through the crowded ballroom. The level of fun and excitement was rising, and the music grew louder to combat it.

They stepped outside and the door closed behind them, muting the sound but not silencing it. The music followed them as they headed up the walk toward the low row of rooms. They took a right turn in the direction of the boathouse. The night was cloudy and blustery and Gina had forgotten her wrap in the dining room.

Patrick pulled off his tux jacket and put in on her shoulders. "I'm surprised you didn't wear the leather jacket tonight," he teased.

She smiled up at him, that bittersweet quality still there. "I was thinking of sewing pearls onto it so I can wear it on formal occasions. But you do still grab it once in a while. You'd probably have difficulty explaining the pearls to the guys you go fishing with."

He put an arm around her shoulders as they headed for the boathouse. "Tell you what. Consider it a gift. I formally turn over ownership of the disputed leather jacket to you."

Gina stopped, frozen on the slab-stone walk. "Why?" she asked. Was it a parting gift?

He squeezed her closer as he urged her on. "Why not? I thought you liked it."

She stopped him again and pulled him under one of the old ornate lights that lit the path to the water. Beyond, in the darkness, water lapped and a freighter blasted its horn to call for a bar pilot. She looked up into his eyes, straining to see what he felt.

"What are you saying?" she demanded.

He frowned at her. "That you can have the jacket. Why? Am I speaking in code?"

"To go *where* in it?"

He rolled his eyes, wondering why this always happened. She often made him feel as though he needed an interpreter. "It doesn't come with restrictions," he replied. "You may go where you like in it."

"With or without you?"

He was beginning to understand. That bittersweet look in her eyes had become desperation, and suddenly what he'd brought her out to tell her had finally, unequivocally lost its power to threaten him. It was hard to be afraid of your own love when it glowed from your woman's eyes.

He folded his arms and grinned down at her. "Well, how do you prefer to travel?"

Tears stung her throat. "In an old VW bus with you behind the wheel and me feeding you potato chips."

He laughed and wrapped his arms around her, locking her against him. "Then that's how we'll spend every anniversary," he said tenderly, lowering his head to kiss her lips. "We'll pack up the old red bus and take off down the coast."

"*Every* anniversary?" she asked. "Like there'll be more than an eleven-month one?"

He framed her face in his hands and let her see how much he loved her before he spoke the words. "God, I hope there'll be sixty or seventy. I hope we set a record. I love you, Gina. I hope you're prepared for this marriage to last a lifetime."

"Oh, Patrick." She melted against him with a softness that turned his spine to mush. "I love you, too." She squeezed him again. "You don't feel obligated . . . ?"

He silenced her with an emphatic kiss. "Look, let's make another deal, all right? You won't try to second-guess what I'm saying if I make a point of trying to put what I'm feeling into words. I love you. Plain and simple." He thought about that a minute, then corrected himself. "Actually, it's not plain at all. It feels kind of baroque and even a little convoluted."

She laughed softly, happy enough to burst. "Sounds like the real thing, all right. I—"

She was interrupted by a tall, slender man in kitchen whites running toward them in the darkness.

He stopped before them, his face sooty, his eyes wide with distress. "The kitchen, Mr. Gallagher!" he shouted. "It's on fire!"

Gina turned to the main building, half expecting to see fire bursting through the windows, but it looked just as it always did, like a beautiful old lady, bejeweled with lights for nighttime.

Patrick turned her in the direction of the ballroom. "Go back to Sin. Tell him what's happened, and don't let any of the guests come back to the main building until I know how bad it is."

"But I want—" She made a move to go with him as he started for the building at a run.

"Go!" He pointed her back to the ballroom, then ran with the sous-chef in pursuit.

Gina hurried to go back to the party, still startled by his admission of love.

"Mrs. Gallagher." The sound of her name jarred Gina. She turned to find the man from Newport

Niceties ambling down the walk from the long arm of the refurbished addition. He was dressed in evening clothes, hands in his pockets.

She smiled. "Good evening. How are you?"

"I'm fine." He pointed in the direction of the small commotion in the doorway of the main building. "Something apparently isn't fine up the way."

"There's a small fire in the kitchen," she said, smiling like a stewardess trying to reassure her concerned passengers. "Nothing to worry about, I'm sure, but I'm going to the ballroom to keep everyone at this end of the complex until we know for sure what's happening."

He caught her arm and corrected her with a faintly disturbing smile. "Actually, there is something to worry about."

There was also something disturbing in his tone.

"I set the fire," he said with a rumbling little laugh. Then he started toward the boathouse, dragging her with him. "Come along, Regina. We have to talk about what you've done with my diamonds."

PATRICK BURST into the kitchen, expecting to find it empty of staff, thick with smoke, a wall burning. But Emil, the chef, was calmly setting up a fan to divert the smoke to the back door, and everyone else was grilling steaks, pulling things out of the oven, slicing *gâteau,* while absently waving a light fog of smoke from their faces.

"No, we did not overdo ze flambé," Emil said with a roll of his eyes as he noticed Patrick. He directed the sous-chef to see that the fan was properly placed and all the windows opened and took Patrick's arm to lead him to the small room off the kitchen where dishes were done and trash disposed of.

There the walls were blackened, and a heavy pall of smoke still hung in the air. Here, too, a fan had been set up. Two waiters wearing napkins over their mouths were cleaning up. Emil led Patrick to an area in the back, walled with cinder blocks, where the trash was kept. One of the large trash containers usually kept in the clean-up area was soggy from having been doused with a pot of pasta water.

"What happened?" Patrick demanded.

"Ze trash went 'poof!'" Emil said, making an exploding gesture with his hands. "Ze flames were very high. Must be somezing smoldered in ze bottom of ze can, but we are very careful with ze paper trash."

"One of the staff got careless with a cigarette?"

"*Mais, non!* No one smokes in my kitchen. Zey know I would guillotine them."

"Then what happened?"

Sin burst out of the kitchen's back door, breathless. "Patrick. Got to talk to you."

Patrick looked up at Sin in mild annoyance. "Sin, we've had a fire here—"

"So did the hotel down the coast, remember?" Sin pointed out. "Little too coincidental, don't you think?"

Emil said something emphatic in French. Patrick frowned. He'd been so concerned about the safety of his staff and guests, he hadn't made the connection. "My call from Watters just came through," Sin went on. "Guess who's here as part of the Northcoast Antique Dealers?"

An icy ripple of foreboding ran down Patrick's back. "Gardner," he asked, "or Danforth?"

"Danforth, registered as Dan Porter. Owns a shop called—" he raised an eyebrow significantly "—Newport Niceties. It's him. Watters faxed me a photo."

Patrick had a clear picture in his mind of the affable man whom Gina always seemed to run into in the strangest places.

"Did you leave Gina at the ballroom?" Patrick asked.

Sin looked confused. "She left with you."

The chill now went up Patrick's spine. "I sent her back when James came to tell me about the fire."

Sin's confusion turned to distress. "I wasn't there. The desk sent someone to tell me Watters's call had come through."

Patrick grabbed Sin's arm and started pulling him with him as he backed away. "Emil, I want everyone in security looking for Mrs. Gallagher," he said.

"But what—"

"Just have them find her and hold her! I don't want them to let her out of their sight. Come on, Sin."

They raced for the ballroom where news of the kitchen fire hadn't reached, or if it had, hadn't dampened the party spirit. The music and the laughter were still loud and fast.

Patrick looked over the room, praying that his eyes would fall on Gina, safe and sound in some guest's arms. But she wasn't there. He did another quick scan of the room, his heart fisting into cold resolve when he still didn't find her.

Patrick spotted Bobbi, dancing with a guest. He had spun her away from him in a daring twirl, and she flew out, colliding with Sin with a gasp of alarm and a swirl of red taffeta skirt.

They stared at each other for a moment, unmoving. Impatiently Patrick grabbed Bobbi's arm and pulled her toward him.

"Where's Gina?" he demanded.

She looked at him blankly. "Well . . . she left with you."

"Oh, God," he muttered. It was suddenly all too clear.

Patrick left the ballroom at a run, Sin and Bobbi close behind him.

THE BOATHOUSE was dark and cold, the lap of the water in the slip a curiously languid sound in an atmosphere tight with anger and quiet panic. Gina's arm was twisted up behind her, her strained shoulder a hot throb of pain. She'd lost Patrick's jacket somewhere in Danforth's headlong rush to get out of sight.

"Now." Danforth shoved her against the wall. She landed with a jarring thud, trying desperately to make her mind work despite the fear. She turned to face her captor, rotating her painful shoulder and making every effort to appear calm.

"What have you done with the diamonds?" Danforth demanded, keeping the distance of a few feet between them. His voice, deep and quiet, closed the small space and crawled over her like something alive.

She tossed her head to shake the feeling. "Why would I," she asked reasonably, "have diamonds that belong to you?"

He heaved a deep sigh. "Regina, don't do this," he said quietly. "You have to have them. Gardner insists that he left the lamp in the warehouse. But when I went to pick it up, it was gone. You have it."

"The lamp?" Gina said in surprise. "You don't mean the lovers'—"

"I do."

"But it's just plaster and—" Suddenly she had a clear mental picture of the crystal drops that sparkled like stars in the firelight.

Danforth came to within a foot of her, the elegant planes of his face a blotch of ugly shadow in the darkness. "So, you *didn't* know," he said in mocking amazement. "Yale took the piece apart and replaced the crystals in the plastic bag you had them packed in, in the warehouse. Didn't you wonder that such an ugly lamp should have such finely cut crystals?"

She hadn't, she thought with a fatal sense of her own naïveté. Until she'd brought it along with her on the trip, she hadn't had much time to look at it. She'd stored it, waiting to refinish it.

She shook her head. "I've never worn diamonds. I like simple gold, myself. You worked for Yale?" she asked.

Danforth snickered. "Yale worked for me. He piled up some gambling debts. I leant him the money to get out from under, and when he couldn't pay me back, I suggested we might...move some merchandise together. I've done this successfully for years. I have many collectors who'll pay a high price for special pieces whose market route they never question."

"The Ming," she whispered. "The Renoir and—"

"And a diamond necklace." In a move made more shocking because of his indolent voice, Danforth grabbed a fistful of her hair and yanked her to the water's edge. "What have you done with the stones?"

"How do you know," she asked, having to swallow to get the words out against her strained throat, "that Yale *doesn't* have it? I...certainly wouldn't take his word."

He shook his head and smiled. "I found him at the airport, about to make his getaway. After what I did to him, I'm sure he told me the truth. He was smart enough to leave me my share before trying to disappear. Now, come on," he said almost amiably, "do I have to do the same to you?"

He yanked her violently to her knees. Pain exploded in her legs at the impact, and her scalp stung from the pressure of his fist in her hair. "Now, where are they?"

She couldn't tell him. She didn't want that animal setting one foot inside Patrick's house.

"I . . . sold it at a little second-hand shop in Burbank," she said in what she prayed was a convincing tone. "Where I sold the rest of the things Yale left in the warehouse."

"You sold it," he repeated in that soft, menacing voice. Then he gave her a vicious shove that landed her in the slip.

Gina drew cold, brackish water into her mouth and her nostrils. Real panic closed in on her as she tried to surface and Danforth's strong hand held her head under. For an interminable moment all attempts to think clearly were swept away as her lungs threatened to burst.

Then the hand that had held her down yanked her up by her hair. Gasping for breath, she clung to the deck of the slip.

"You didn't sell it," he said as she choked and gasped for air. "Yale assured me you had a sentimental attachment to it. It wasn't on the invoice of things you sold that little shop. I checked." His voice lowered as he crouched down to get nose to nose with her. "And security's too tight around here for me to try to check your house. Is that where it is? Somewhere in your cozy little Victorian love nest? If I don't get the right answer this time," he said in an infuriated whisper as he straightened, "your body's going to wash up somewhere in Cannon Beach! Now where is—?"

There was a hollow thud, then Danforth sailed over her head with a high, shrill cry, arcing into the water with a loud splash. Wiping water from her face, Gina found herself being hauled up by two rescuers she didn't recognize in the dark.

One gave the other a quick shove. "Go find Mr. Gallagher!" a young man's voice said urgently. She recognized it as Brian's. "Hurry!"

"But . . ." Katey's voice.

"Hurry!"

Katey ran off as Brian hauled Gina onto the deck. Then he pushed her to follow Katey. "Go!" he said. "I'll take care of him."

But Danforth rose out of the water swearing and spitting and promising Brian an ugly death. Gina knew what Danforth was capable of. She couldn't leave Brian. She searched around frantically for a weapon, but there was nothing. So she stood beside Brian, waiting for Danforth, who'd wisely leapt out of the water on the other side of the boathouse.

"Mrs. Gallagher!" Brian said impatiently, trying to push her toward the door. But Danforth was too close and Brian quickly changed tactics. He pushed Gina behind him and began to back away.

"All right!" Danforth roared, advancing on them as water streamed off him. "I've *had* it!" The dip in the water seemed to have shaken his calm. "Do you have any idea what you've put me through? Do you?'' he demanded. ''I've wasted weeks of valuable time, had a forty-five thousand dollar car disabled, two men thrown in jail—''

''Car disabled?'' Gina leaned around Brian to scoff. ''It was only a distributor cap! You're not much of a mechanic, are you? And your henchmen are pathetic.''

''Mrs. Gallagher!'' Brian pleaded desperately, trying to push her back behind him.

''I'm very good,'' Danforth said, picking up his pace toward them, ''at getting rid of what gets in my way. Now getting you out of my hair has come to mean almost more to me than the diamonds!'' And he lunged at them.

Chapter Fourteen

Gina could only hear the tussle. She'd landed at the bottom of the pile like a running back who'd been dumped at the Super Bowl.

It occurred to her that it seemed inordinately loud for a two-man scuffle, then she heard Patrick's voice, then Sin's and Bobbi's and Katey's.

When Patrick hauled her to her feet, Danforth lay on the deck, mouth open, eyes closed.

Patrick wrapped her in Sin's jacket, tucking it high around her neck. "Gina, are you all right?" he demanded.

She felt his cold hand against her face, felt her body trembling wildly under the warm jacket. She was aware of being very cold and vaguely disoriented. Patrick was holding her close and rubbing her arm and back. Bobbi was studying her worriedly.

"I'm fine," she said in a voice that surprised her with its strength. She certainly didn't feel strong.

Then the men from security appeared with flashlights and weapons and Danforth was taken away.

Brian gave the assembled group a blow-by-blow description of everything he and Katey had heard and seen from inside the cruiser.

"What were you doing in the cruiser?" Bobbi asked, obviously puzzled.

Sin rolled his eyes.

"We were, ah, making wedding plans," Brian said, clearing his throat.

Patrick gave him a hearty hug with his free hand. "Thank God for wedding plans. You two go back to the hotel. I'm sure the police will want to talk to you. Sin will go to my place to turn over the stones."

Sin nodded.

Patrick held Gina closer. "I'm taking Gina to the emergency room."

"I think that's an excellent idea," Bobbi said.

Gina struggled feebly, trying to rouse herself out of her woolly state. She felt fine. The only problem seemed to be with her brain. She could almost hear it slowing down, clouding over.

Gina said firmly to her friend, "I'm fine."

Bobbi folded her arms. "It wouldn't hurt to have a doctor make sure, would it?"

The faces around Gina began to recede, and the beam of the flashlight the security team had left with them began to undulate. She summoned her waning energy to say emphatically, "I do *not* want to go to the doctor." Then counteracted all that effort by fainting dead away.

GINA AWOKE in the emergency room as a middle-aged woman, glasses perched halfway down her nose, took her blood pressure. A badge on the pocket of the woman's lab coat said she was Dr. Davidson.

She pulled the stethoscope from her ears and dropped it around her neck, smiling at Gina as she did so. "Good. You're both fine. I understand you've had quite an evening."

"*Both* fine?" Gina asked, trying to surface to full brain capacity. "Patrick!" she said in sudden alarm. "Was my husband hurt?" She couldn't quite bring back the details that had brought her here. She remembered being frightened, being in the water, fainting. But Patrick had seemed fine.

Then he came from behind her to stand beside the doctor. He appeared in perfect health.

"Oh!" Gina put a hand to her heart in relief. His declaration of love came back to her, those few wonderful moments on the walk before James came from the kitchen to report the fire. She smiled at him, love bright in her eyes.

His expression remained carefully neutral, something remote and vaguely angry in his eyes. Gina stared at him, confused.

"By *both of you*," the doctor said, reclaiming her attention, "I meant you and the baby."

"What baby?"

Dr. Davidson turned to Patrick, then back to Gina with a concerned, maternal smile. "*Your* baby, Gina. Didn't you know?"

Gina felt her mouth gape. She slowly shook her head. Then she smiled as she dealt with a flash of ebullience. A baby!

Her eyes flew to Patrick's, and the smile died on her face as she finally interpreted his curiously remote expression. He'd obviously learned the news before she'd come to. He probably thought she'd done it deliberately, that allowing herself to get pregnant had been a ploy to keep him in the marriage once she'd reached her birthday.

She must have gotten pregnant one of the first few times they'd made love—long before he'd declared his love and while he was still adamant about not wanting to father her child. He must think she'd tricked him—again.

Dr. Davidson looked from one to the other. "I know this hasn't been the ideal way to find out such happy news," she said gently. "Maybe you should go home and start this evening all over again in the light of what you know now."

She swung Gina's legs over the side of the gurney. "You had a very normal reaction to the circumstances." She looked up at Patrick. "She should lie low for a few days—maybe just rest through the holiday. By Tuesday, she should be good as new."

Patrick nodded, gave Gina a quick, cursory glance and handed her a pile of clothes.

She recognized a pink sweat suit from her closet and looked at him in confusion.

"Sin and Bobbi brought them," he said stiffly, "so you could change out of the wet dress. I'll be in the waiting room while you get dressed."

GINA PRETENDED interest in downtown Astoria as Patrick drove through it toward the bridge that would take them back to Candle Bay. At just after one in the morning all the shops and businesses were closed. Her mind made a quick parallel between this drive and the part of the trip where she'd awakened just outside of San Francisco at about the same hour of the morning. It was shortly after that that they'd found the barn and the hayloft—then found each other. Now she was about to lose him.

She didn't know what to say. He hadn't spoken a word to her since he'd put her in the Firebird he drove when he wasn't hauling building materials.

God, she thought unhappily. Was everything she'd gained a few hours ago about to fall apart because of a misunderstanding?

Patrick knew precisely what he wanted to say, but he needed time to calm down. Had her surprise at the news been an act? Had she not even suspected she was pregnant? Or had she known and kept it to herself so that if it all did fall apart between them she'd have what she wanted without interference from him?

Part of him found that hard to believe of her, but another part remembered that she'd lied to him before.

As he drove onto the bridge, the only car on the road, he glanced her way. She looked pale and small wrapped in the blanket he'd given her, and very miserable.

He'd forgotten until that moment what she'd been through tonight. From the time she'd fainted in his arms, he'd handled more fear than he'd ever felt in combat.

He kept his eyes on the lights of his hotel in the distance, trying to find an answer to his questions. All he could see in his mind's eye was her laughing beside him in the passenger seat of the truck, then the old bus, talking chattily, nibbling constantly on chips or cookies. Then he remembered her putting herself between him and Larry's gun. Held against his suspicions, nothing computed.

He pulled into a lay-by off the road where tourists stopped during the day to look at the sights of Astoria, and where lovers stopped at night to look into each other's eyes.

He turned the motor off, and silence boomed in the small space of the car. He stared through the windshield for a slow count of ten, then turned to her.

"Explain to me," he said quietly, "what's happened here."

Gina felt like she might burst from the joy and the fear warring within her for supremacy. She was ecstatic that she was pregnant, but she knew that the reason for her delight could also cause her to lose Patrick.

She turned to him with a smile because she was simply unable to dredge up any guilt. "It's called life," she said. "It's the result of love."

He couldn't dispute that. "What I want to know," he said, "is how did it happen? I thought you were protected."

"So did I." She pulled the blanket tighter around her.

"How could you have no idea you were pregnant? The doctor guessed you to be about six weeks along. There are signs—"

"I've just been moving too fast, I guess," she said, shrugging so that the blanket rose and fell. "I haven't counted days because I wasn't worried about it. I thought I was safe. I had a little mild nausea, but I put it down to nerves."

Her face was alive with excitement, happiness, trepidation and concern. But she was absolutely sincere; he was sure of it.

Gina found him difficult to read. Impatient because she didn't know what to think, she said moodily, "Undoubtedly this will be a baby that makes a lot of noise, eats you out of house and home, and draws trouble like a magnet. Not a convenient distraction for a busy innkeeper."

He made a small sound of amusement. "Noise, food and trouble sort of define our relationship. It's probably been the most inconvenient marriage of convenience on record."

"And I guess that's *my* fault?"

He shrugged a shoulder. "You're the one who tricked me into this, was responsible for the fact that we were chased a thousand miles, and placed a half-million-dollar lamp on our mantel that put us both in danger." With a trace of a smile, he continued. "I don't see how you can blame anyone else."

Anger rose in her like fire up a draft. "Oh, really! Well, let me tell you a thing or two!"

She rounded on him. He braced himself. He'd hear her out, and then he'd tell how it was going to be.

"Everything is your fault, Patrick," she said emphatically, dropping the blanket to allow herself free use of restless hands. She stabbed one in his direction. "Had we done it my way in the beginning, we'd have gotten along just fine, made a baby and gone our separate ways. But no!"

The same hand swiped in his direction to reinforce the negative. "You had to be all tough and noble and responsible!"

He thought that through. Toughness could be debatable as a virtue, but weren't nobility and responsibility sought after in a man by most women?

Her eyes filled. "You had to be brave and concerned and fun. You had to make love to me in a damned hayloft!"

He smiled and put a hand to her face. "Now, I wasn't solely responsible for that. You sat there on a moonbeam looking like an angel. What was I supposed to do?"

"It's just possible..." she began heatedly, then hesitated when his words played over in her mind. Like an angel? Refusing to be distracted, she gave her hair a toss and began again. "It's just possible you could come to love this baby, but if you don't want to give yourself the chance, it's fine with me."

"I'm thrilled about the baby," he said, his tone annoyed because he was mad at *her*. She was second-guessing him again. "I love it already."

She stared at him, afraid to believe him. "I don't want you to love it because you feel obligated," she said.

Patrick closed his eyes, shook his head and turned the key in the ignition. That did it.

"I've been there," she said. "And my baby will not grow up having just half of her father's attention."

He backed onto the road and roared toward the inn. "It isn't *your* baby, it's our baby, and you're second-guessing me again. Have you ever had only half of my attention, except when you were being a pill? Like now?"

When she didn't answer, he cast her a quick, dark glance. "Then just shut up about it until we get to the office."

She subsided in her blanket. "Why are we going to the office?"

"We're going to do what the doctor suggested," he said. "We're going to start this evening over in the light of what we know now." He pulled into the spot marked with his name and turned to her and warned quietly, "And you'd better get it right, Mrs. Gallagher. Come on."

He pulled her out of the car, blanket and all, and strode to the side entrance of the main building with her in his arms.

The grounds were quiet now, though the ballroom was still brightly lit.

He stopped at the door to his office, propped one knee against the wall, balanced her on it and unlocked his door. He put her on her feet in front of his desk, turning on the low light on the credenza in the corner. The soft light did not interfere with the glittering view of the ballroom and Astoria beyond the bay.

He took the blanket from her, tossed it in a corner and positioned her before the window where she'd been earlier that evening when he'd walked out of the bathroom.

He stepped back a few steps, reaching out to turn her back to the window when she tried to follow him.

"We're going to recreate this evening," he said. "Only this time we're going to do it better. Do you remember how it went?"

"I remember every minute of how it's gone," she said without turning away from the window, "from the day you opened the door in my father's study and found me standing there."

"Good," he said. "Then you're on. I've just closed the bathroom door."

Gina drew a deep breath, then turned to look at him over her shoulder. "Hi," she said, her voice barely there. She cleared her throat and said it again. "It looks like something out of *Ali Baba,* doesn't it?"

Patrick moved to stand behind her, thinking how beautiful she looked in the sweats, with her hair a mess. He ached with love.

"It does," he replied, putting a hand on her arm as he'd done earlier, fighting the urge to crush her to him. "Do you feel like Scheherazade?" He turned her to him. "Or are you Aladdin with your unconventional lamp?"

"I have a thousand-and-one tales to tell you," she whispered, feeling choked with what she saw in his eyes. He did love her and their baby. All the doubt had been hers.

He put a hand to her face. "To tell you, *O Sultan,*" he prompted with a grin. "I really liked that part."

"To tell you, O Sultan," she laughed softly. But instead of leading him away as she had earlier, she pushed him gently into the deep chair behind his desk. They *were* going to do this right this time. "The first is a long and complicated one," she said.

He pulled her into his lap. "Then go slowly, wife."

She settled comfortably against the arm that held her and thought back to their almost fairy-tale beginning. "There was a mighty sultan," she began, "who took a vizier's daughter to wife."

Patrick nodded sagely. "A tale of woe."

Gina scolded him with a look. "A tale of love."

"Ah," he said. "Continue."

"The sultan and his wife began a perilous journey on a magic carpet. Thieves were in pursuit, for the sultan's wife had a magic lamp."

"Were they overtaken?"

"Very nearly. To escape they were forced to trade the magic carpet for a very slow camel."

Patrick kept a straight face with difficulty.

"But the sultan and his wife," Gina went on, putting a finger to his lips, "were as much in peril from each other as from the thieves."

He kissed her fingertip, then pulled her hand down. "Why was that?"

"The survival of his kingdom," she replied, "and her personal safety depended on their close alliance. But he was a leader of men and sheltered his person, like his people, in a fortress. His wife was taught by the vizier, her father, that love is painful if not returned."

He combed a wisp of her hair back with his fingertips. She stared out the window, her voice quiet and haunting as she continued.

"And so they mated during the starry desert nights, each thinking the heart could be held apart from the body. When they reached the sultan's palace, his soldiers captured the thieves and threw them into the bowels of the palace."

"And the sultan and his wife lived together to a happy old age?"

Gina leaned her head on Patrick's shoulder and sighed. "The sultan discovered that his wife was with child," she said. "He thought it was a trick to make her more important to him than his other wives."

"Other wives?" Patrick asked.

"One wife in particular," she said, "was very large and very powerful and demanded his attention."

"Mmm. I hope he was wise enough to see the treasure he had in the vizier's daughter."

Gina leaned her elbow on his shoulder and looked into his eyes. "This is where the tale grows weak."

"I know this story," Patrick said, sinking deeper into the chair and pushing her head gently back to his shoulder. "Shall I conclude?"

Gina snuggled into him and closed her eyes and prayed.

"Despite the noise made by the large wife," he said, a smile in his voice, "he remembered all the pleasures the vizier's daughter had given him. He remembered the balm of her laughter, the sustenance her gentle ways provided, the whiteness of her body in the moonlight and its generosity always." He was silent a moment, then went on quietly. "Their child would be a part of them, and the sum total of their special singularity."

Gina raised her head, tears streaming down her face and kissed him desperately, ardently.

"You want the baby?" she whispered. "Honestly?"

"Of course I do. The only thing that worried me was that you knew and hadn't told me so that you could leave with it if anything went wrong."

"I didn't know. And I'd have never done that to you."

He tucked her knees up higher and crossed his feet on the windowsill. He turned the chair so that they could see the glittery reflection of Astoria in Candle Bay.

"The sultan—" he picked up the threads of the story to tie them off "—ordered feasting and dancing. He gave his wife a necklace of pearls and put the lamp in a place of honor in the palace because keeping it safe had brought them great love."

"He placed it in their chamber window," Gina corrected, "so that whenever he left the palace, it would shine for him like her love and call him home."

Patrick laughed softly and kissed her forehead. "You're getting your Scheherazade and your Polly Dutton stories all mixed up."

"No." Gina pointed to the glimmer of light visible from their bedroom window in the uppermost corner of the office windowpane. "It's *our* story, and the middle of my rainbow." She wrapped her arms around his neck and kissed him.

◆ **H A R L E Q U I N**

A Calendar of Romance

Our most magical month is here! December—thirty-one days of carolers and snowmen, and thirty-one nights of hot cider and roaring fires. Come in from the cold, get cozy and cuddle with a Christmas cowboy and snuggle with a magic man. Celebrate Christmas and Hanukkah next month with American Romance's four Calendar of Romance titles:

Happy Holidays

DECEMBER

M		W	T	F	S
		2	3	4	5
		9	10	11	12
13	14	15	16	17	18	19
20	21	22	23	24	25	26
27	28	29	30	31	

#465
A CHRISTMAS
MARRIAGE
by Dallas Schulze

#466
A COWBOY
FOR CHRISTMAS
by Anne McAllister

#467
SWEET LIGHT
by Judith Arnold

#468
A COUNTRY
CHRISTMAS
by Jackie Weger

Make the most romantic month even more romantic!

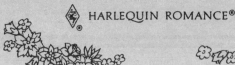 

HARLEQUIN ROMANCE®

**Harlequin Romance
has love in
store for you!**

Don't miss next
month's title in

THE BRIDAL COLLECTION

A WHOLESALE ARRANGEMENT
by Day Leclaire

THE BRIDE *needed* the Groom.
THE GROOM *wanted* the Bride.
BUT THE WEDDING was *more* than
a convenient solution!

Available this month in
The Bridal Collection
Only Make-Believe
by Bethany Campbell
Harlequin Romance #3230

HE CROSSED TIME FOR HER

Captain Richard Colter rode the high seas, brandished a sword and pillaged treasure ships. A swashbuckling privateer, he was a man with voracious appetites and a lust for living. And in the eighteenth century, any woman swooned at his feet for the favor of his wild passion. History had it that Captain Richard Colter went down with his ship, the *Black Cutter,* in a dazzling sea battle off the Florida coast in 1792.

Then what was he doing washed ashore on a Key West beach in 1992—alive?

MARGARET ST. GEORGE brings you an extraspecial love story this month, about an extraordinary man who would do anything for the woman he loved:

#462 THE PIRATE AND HIS LADY
by Margaret St. George

When love is meant to be, nothing can stand in its way . . . not even time.

Don't miss American Romance
#462 THE PIRATE AND HIS LADY.
It's a love story you'll never forget.

PAL-A

HARLEQUIN ROMANCE®

After her father's heart attack, Stephanie Bloomfield comes home to Orchard Valley, Oregon, to be with him and with her sisters.

Orchard Valley

Steffie learns that many things have changed in her absence—but not her feelings for journalist Charles Tomaselli. He was the reason she left Orchard Valley. Now, three years later, will he give her a reason to stay?

"The Orchard Valley trilogy features three delightful, spirited sisters and a trio of equally fascinating men. The stories are rich with the romance, warmth of heart and humor readers expect, and invariably receive, from Debbie Macomber."

—Linda Lael Miller

Don't miss the Orchard Valley trilogy by Debbie Macomber:

Look for the special cover flash on each book!

Available wherever Harlequin books are sold.